The Legend of FIRE

Lee Roddy

F...
Pomo...

THE LEGEND OF FIRE

Copyright © 1988 by Lee Roddy

Library of Congress Cataloging in Publication Data

Roddy, Lee, 1921—
  The legend of fire.

  (A Ladd family adventure)
  Summary: A young Christian inadvertently places his family in danger on
Hawaii's Kona Coast when he videotapes the dramatic rescue of two drowning
children which leads to his father's kidnapping.
  [1. Kidnapping—Fiction. 2. Hawaii—Fiction. 3. Christian life—Fiction]
I. Title. II. Series:
Roddy, Lee, 1921—   . Ladd family adventure.
PZ7.R6Le 1988 [Fic]   88-24292
ISBN 0-929608-17-8

Published by Focus on the Family Publishing, Pomona, CA 91799.

Distributed by Word Books, Waco, Texas.

Scripture quotations are taken from the Revised Standard Version of the Bible
© Copyright 1982, Holman Bible Publishers.

Editor: Janet Kobobel
Designer: Sherry Nicolai Russell
Cover Illustration: Ernest Norcia

Printed in the United States of America

89 90 91 92 93 / 10 9 8 7 6 5 4 3 2

To Jack Bliler,
my first city editor,
who patiently gave me the
opportunity to develop my skills
on the long road
to writing fulfillment

CONTENTS

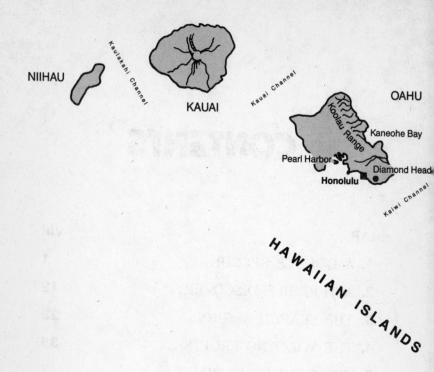

NIIHAU

Kaulakahi Channel

KAUAI

Kauai Channel

OAHU

Koolau Range

Kaneohe Bay

Pearl Harbor

Diamond Head

Honolulu

Kaiwi Channel

HAWAIIAN ISLANDS

Pacific Ocean

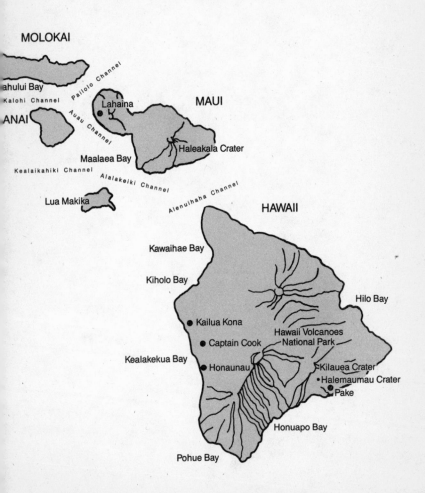

Pacific Ocean

MOLOKAI

ahului Bay

Kalohi Channel

Pailolo Channel

ANAI

Auau Channel

Lahaina

MAUI

Maalaea Bay

Haleakala Crater

Kealaikahiki Channel

Alalakeiki Channel

Lua Makika

Alenuihaha Channel

HAWAII

Kawaihae Bay

Kiholo Bay

Hilo Bay

Kailua Kona

Captain Cook

Hawaii Volcanoes
National Park

Kealakekua Bay

Honaunau

Kilauea Crater

Halemaumau Crater

Pake

Honuapo Bay

Pohue Bay

Chapter One

A DOUBLE RESCUE

It happened so suddenly that Josh Ladd missed the first part. Stretched out on a straw mat, he was sunbathing on his back when he heard a strange sound, like a faint cry for help.

He sat up abruptly, squinting with his intense blue eyes at the vast expanse of the Pacific Ocean in front of him. At first, he saw nothing except the surf glistening in the late afternoon sun off the nearly deserted beach on the south coast of the Big Island of Hawaii.

The ocean was quiet, as though it were resting. Then it rose like the chest of a giant taking a deep breath, and a wave formed a black mass against the skyline. The wave grew bigger and bigger, then seemed to stop and hang in midair. Slowly, then faster and faster, the wave collapsed in on itself and rolled toward the white sandy beach where Josh sat. It hit the hidden lava reef beneath the surface, flattened and lost power. Then it flung itself like an exhausted swimmer onto the shore and dissolved into a white cover of hissing foam.

1

That's when Josh saw something moving in the water. He straightened automatically on his mat and stared hard. He was big for his twelve years, with strong arms and wide shoulders.

There! In the deep blue trough of water fifty feet off-shore. Two seals? A couple of sea otters? No, he had seen those often enough when he lived in California, but those creatures didn't play off Hawaii's shores.

He turned to the left where his father and mother were reading under a multicolored beach umbrella. As he moved, Josh brushed against his father's video camera that he had placed in the shade of his body after shooting some footage of the family. His favorite dream was to one day own a camera and take pictures all over the islands.

"Dad," Josh called out over the ocean sounds, "what's that in the water?"

Both parents lowered their books and looked where Josh pointed. Before they could answer, Josh saw a young man leap up from the sand, drop a pair of binoculars and grab a fluorescent orange, torpedo-shaped object about three feet long.

Then Josh realized that the man was a powerful-looking native beach guard. His nose looked strangely white where he had placed zinc oxide cream to protect his skin from the sun. He wore bright orange nylon swim trunks with a Red Cross patch sewn to the right leg.

Slipping a loop of rope that was attached to the lightweight torpedo over his shoulder, the beach guard scooped up the fluorescent orange buoy and sprinted toward the surf.

Josh's mother exclaimed, "What on earth...?"

"Possible drowning!" her husband replied, leaping from under the umbrella's shade.

That's when Josh realized what was happening.

As he jumped up, he could see clearly that the two dark objects in the water were humans, waving frantically. Their mouths moved, but Josh couldn't hear their cries above the surf's sound.

He saw the powerfully built beach guard running fast, bronze legs pumping, splashing into the water.

Then he heard his mother ask anxiously, "Oh, John, can he save them both?"

"Probably not." His father's voice was sharp with tension. "He can only save one at a time."

"John! What're you doing?"

Josh glanced in sudden fear at his father, who had jerked off his silver-framed half-glasses. In the same movement, he bent down and snatched up a long green beach towel. Then he sprinted across the sand after the racing beach guard.

Josh's mouth went dry with fear. "Oh, Dad!" It was a moan; a prayer.

Josh could hear his older sister and little brother yelling and knew they had seen what was going on. They were running toward the scene from the lava tidal pools where they had been playing.

Josh understood what was going to happen in the ocean. His father, a tall, wide-chested man with dark, wavy hair, had coached swimming for a while during his high school history-teaching days in California. He had earned his water safety instructor rating when he was eighteen and still had it. Josh had already started on the same long, hard road by earning his junior lifesaving rating this year.

Without really thinking about what he was doing, Josh reacted to his long-time love of photography by picking up the video camera. Settling it on his shoulder, he closed one eye and squinted through the viewfinder with the other eye. It was a fully automatic camera so that Josh didn't have to focus or take light readings. He simply pushed a thumb button. A red light winked on. The black microphone at the front of the camera recorded sound while the videotape began rolling.

"Mom! What's happening?" Josh's fourteen-year-old sister Tiffany screamed. "Where's Dad going?"

Josh didn't hear his mother's answer. Instead, he concentrated on keeping the camera steady. Two years ago, his father had taught him the importance of moving the camera slowly; panning steadily, without jerking.

Through the viewfinder, Josh saw the beach guard dive into deep water. He swam powerfully through the surf, the torpedo buoy trailing on the rope. Almost at once, John Ladd dove in behind him, the long beach towel stuffed in his waistband so he could have both hands free to swim.

Several feet short of the nearest victim, the guard suddenly stopped swimming. He threw himself over on his back so his head and hands were out of reach of the wildly thrashing victim. Slipping the rope off his shoulder, the beach guard shoved the far end of the buoy toward the drowning person.

Josh knew the guard was trying to reassure the person and then giving orders to grab the end of the buoy. The victim willingly obeyed. Studying the scene through the camera, Josh exclaimed, "It's a little girl!"

He saw the guard turn and head back toward shore, swimming strongly and towing the exhausted girl. She had collapsed across the torpedo buoy.

Josh opened his other eye to locate his father. He also suddenly reversed his body and stopped just out of the second victim's flailing reach. Josh leveled the camera at Mr. Ladd as he threw one end of the wet towel to the second person, a boy.

Josh knew his father was repeating the guard's assurances and instructions. The second victim was too panicked to listen. He grabbed the end of the towel thrown to him, but it wasn't stiff and reassuring like the buoy. Frantically pulling hand over hand on the limp towel, he desperately reached for his rescuer's head.

"Look out, Dad!" Josh yelled, lowering the camera. He knew the first rule of life guarding: "Don't let the victim get his hands on you. He could drown you both."

John Ladd was too experienced to let that happen. He

tucked his chin in tightly against his left shoulder to protect his windpipe and grabbed the struggling child's wrists. He made a sudden movement that spun the victim around. The two disappeared under the water.

When they surfaced, the boy had stopped struggling. John Ladd reached around the victim's shoulder from behind and gripped him by the chin with one hand. Then Mr. Ladd began swimming toward shore, using his right arm and a scissors kick.

Josh remembered the camera and raised it to his eye. The red light was still on. The beach guard was just coming ashore with the person he had rescued, and Josh's father was a few feet behind.

As he also touched bottom and stood up, still holding the boy, Josh released the button. Setting the camera down on the reed mat, he joined his mother, sister and brother in rushing toward the water.

John Ladd and the beach guard examined the two near-drowning victims. Both were conscious and able to move. The girl whom the beach guard had brought ashore was about ten, the age of Josh's little brother, Nathan. The other was a boy about Josh's age. They were too frightened and weak to talk.

Spectators ran up from nowhere. One was an upset young woman who was obviously their baby sitter. "I only took my eyes off them for a minute! They were on their board—"

Josh's father interrupted. "Someone call an ambulance."

It soon arrived with two uniformed officers following in a patrol car. While the children were taken to a hospital for observation, one officer took the baby sitter's statement and the other questioned the beach guard and Josh's father.

By the time it was all over, darkness had settled. The Ladd family got into their rented car and drove back to their hotel room in Kailua-Kona, an ancient Hawaiian city modernized for tourists who loved the warm south coast.

Everyone was too excited to eat. Except for their father, who had made half a dozen rescues in his lifetime, the rest of the Ladds had never seen anything like this. But the beach guard had told them he averaged more than two hundred saves each year. It wasn't the kind of publicity the islanders wanted to share with their millions of annual visitors, although signs on various beaches warned against possible drowning hazards.

"It's probably not even going to be on the eleven o'clock news," Josh decided. That was too bad; it would have been fun to hear his father's name mentioned on TV.

Mr. Ladd drove his family around in the soft darkness of early evening until they had exhausted their thoughts on the afternoon's events. Then he brought up the reason the family had come to the Big Island.

"We've pretty well explored the island of Oahu. But tomorrow it's time to start seeing everything we can on the Big Island. What would each of you like to do first?"

"I'd like to see the mountain that's still an active volcano," Mrs. Ladd mused. "Kilauea*, I think it's called. I've got some maps in the hotel room."

As the older sister, Tiffany automatically assumed she could speak for all the kids. "Let's walk in to see the volcano pit; we want to look right down into a real live one!"

Josh objected. "I'd rather start with the Hawaii Volcanoes National Park*. Okay with you, Nathan?"

The youngest Ladd family member was small for his age and towheaded, with lots of freckles that looked like ants running across the bridge of his nose. He alone of the Ladds didn't like Hawaii.

"I don't care about any of them!" Nathan announced. "Let's go find Pele*."

Mr. Ladd glanced into the rear view mirror at his youngest son. "What've you heard about Pele?"

Their father's tone suggested something that made Nathan cautious. "Well, that she's a legend. That's what Tank and Roger said."

Tank Catlett was Josh's best friend, who had moved recently to Hawaii. Roger Okamoto was a third-generation American of Japanese descent. The Ladds, Catletts and Okamotos all lived in apartments on Oahu, at the foot of the famous Honolulu landmark, Diamond Head*.

---

*The definition and pronunciation of words marked by an asterisk are contained in a glossary at the end of the book.

Mrs. Ladd asked, "Nathan, do you know what a legend is?"

"Uh-huh. Something like a story."

"Close enough," his mother agreed. "Actually, it's a story that nobody can prove to be true or false, and it's handed down from one generation to the next. Legends usually involve the supernatural, too, I think. Right, John?"

"Right, dear. Nathan, supernatural means something that can't be explained by natural laws."

"I know. Like ghosts, right?" the little boy asked.

"Well, there are no such things as ghosts, of course, just as Pele doesn't really exist."

"Roger says she does," Josh spoke up. "His grandfather saw her once!"

Tiffany scoffed. "How can anybody see something that doesn't exist?"

Josh became defensive. "I'm just telling you what Roger says. He's no dummy, you know. He's smart!"

"Don't tell me you're starting to believe these Hawaiian legends?" Tiffany demanded. "Like Pele and the Menehunes*."

Nathan piped up. "What's a Menehune?"

"Oh, sort of like little people that don't exist—fairies or Irish leprechauns and elves," Josh explained.

"Well, you've all been in Hawaii long enough to know that this place is loaded with legends," Josh's father said firmly. "Some local people genuinely believe in them, so be careful not to laugh or offend them. It's not polite, even though we know they're just stories."

Mrs. Ladd twisted around in the front seat. "You know what might be fun? To learn something about these legends. Especially the legend of fire."

"What's that?" Nathan asked.

"She means Pele," Tiffany explained. "She's supposed to live in volcanoes."

Nathan's interest sharpened immediately. "In volcanoes? Could they blow up?"

"You mean, 'erupt,'" Josh corrected. "Yes, they could. Roger says Pele causes them to erupt. He says that Pele gets real mad, and she throws molten lava out of the volcanoes. Roger says his grandfather's fishing village was once destroyed because Pele was angry with him."

Tiffany laughed. "Josh, you surprise me! You're starting to sound as if you believe in the locals' legends."

"I didn't say I believe it. I'm just telling you what Roger said."

"That's enough, children!" their mother warned them. "Since we're now residents of this state, let's make it a point to learn something about the cultures of the many ethnic groups that live here, including their legends."

"Like Pele?" Nathan asked excitedly.

"Yes, even Pele," his mother answered.

John Ladd parked the car and led his family into the hotel lobby. As the clerk reached into a cubbyhole for the room key, he handed Mr. Ladd some small yellow notes.

"What's this?" Josh's father asked in surprise. He glanced down while the family gathered around. "All from television stations. They want to interview us for their news! Must be about the rescue; but why's that worth the TV stations' time?"

As the family excitedly discussed what to do, they took the elevator to the sixth floor.

"Can't do any harm," Mr. Ladd declared as they got out of the elevator. "I might even get a chance to mention that I'm trying to buy a weekly newspaper."

"Oh, then maybe we could use a photo from the broadcast on the front page of the first edition!" Tiffany excitedly cried.

Josh snapped his fingers. "Dad! Mom! I just remembered! I've got that whole rescue on videotape!"

Even though no one knew it at the time, that announcement would plunge the whole family into the greatest danger of their lives.

Chapter Two

A TERRIBLE DISCOVERY

In their hotel room, the Ladds gathered excitedly around the video's playback monitor. As the tape rolled by on the one-inch television screen, everyone exclaimed how clear and good it was.

"Your father couldn't have done any better!" Mrs. Ladd reached over and gave Josh a quick hug.

"I could have on that part!" Josh's father said with a chuckle. "When we were coming out of the water, Josh, you must have put down the camera without releasing the button."

Josh agreed. "I thought the camera would stop when I took my thumb off the switch."

"Sounds logical," his father admitted, "but this camera doesn't work that way. It keeps running until the button is pushed to 'Stop.'"

"Hey! Look at the spectators you photographed without even knowing it!"

"Good thing that camera's automatic," Tiffany said with a laugh. "Look how it focused all by itself on that guy."

Josh nodded and watched the bystander move out of the camera's view. "Where you going, Dad?" he asked, as his father rapidly strode across the room.

"To call the television stations. I'm anxious to find out why this near-drowning incident is important enough for them to track me down." Mr. Ladd settled his half-glasses on his nose so he could read the phone number on the slip.

All except Josh left the video camera and clustered around John Ladd while he called the television station in Hilo, a community on the other side of the island. The other stations were in Honolulu, about two hundred miles away.

Josh rewound the tape and ran it again. When it came to the unsuspecting onlooker, the boy frowned. He put the camera on freeze-frame and studied the man.

He was short and dark, and he wore a plain white aloha shirt. It wasn't tucked in, but was worn outside of military-colored pants. His eyes were hard, and there was something cruel about his mouth. Suddenly, Josh straightened up.

"That looks like. . .nah!" he told himself. "Can't be." He turned off the camera. "I wish Tank were here."

Tank Catlett was his best friend. Both boys had grown up together until about a year ago when Tank's father was promoted to manage a chain department store in Honolulu. He and his family had moved to the fiftieth state, leaving Josh terribly lonely until his family had also moved to Hawaii a few weeks ago.

"John Ladd returning your newsroom's call," Josh heard his father say. Then he cupped his hand over the receiver. "I guess they got my name from the police report, but I still can't imagine why they're calling."

Mrs. Ladd suggested, "Maybe the beach guard noticed Josh with the camera and mentioned it to one of the officers."

"Maybe, but I doubt it," Josh said, shaking his head. "He was coming ashore when I stopped shooting and put the camera down."

"If the stations know about the film, will they pay you for it, Dad?" Tiffany asked.

"How many times do you have to be told," Nathan muttered, "it's not film; it's video."

Mrs. Ladd glanced reprovingly at her youngest son. "Nathan, there's no reason to be so critical of your sister."

"Well, everybody knows that you have to develop film, but video's like a tape recorder; it's ready to be played right now."

"Shh!" their father said. "Somebody's coming on the. . .hello! Yes, this is John Ladd."

Josh sighed, turned off the video camera's monitor and stood frowning, looking across at his father.

He was saying, "Oh, now I understand. They're a senator's children."

"I wonder which senator?" Mrs. Ladd asked quietly.

Mr. Ladd held up a hand for silence. "What?" he said into the phone. "Yes, if you feel that it's newsworthy, I'd be happy to have your camera crew come over. Fine.

"Oh, before we hang up, how did you get my name and the hotel where we're staying? Ah, yes! That's what I guessed. I didn't think you were calling about the videotape my son shot of the rescue on our home camera."

Mr. Ladd popped his hand over the receiver and grinned at his family. He whispered, "You should hear his response to that!" He uncovered the mouthpiece.

"Yes, I've just looked at the footage. It's all there; the whole thing. Nice and clear. What? National network and cable release? Well, let's talk about that when you get here."

He hung up the phone. "Can you believe that? Those were Senator DeMott's kids!"

Even Josh recognized the name. The senator was often on television, and some people said he would probably run for president one day.

"Maybe they'll give you a medal, Dad!" Nathan's blue eyes opened wide.

John Ladd laughed and ruffled his son's hair. "I'd rather have that newspaper deal I'm working on come through than get a dozen medals."

He started to reach for the phone to call the other stations just as it rang. At first, Josh thought it was one of the television stations calling back. But seconds after his father picked up the receiver, Josh could see from the look on his face that it was someone else. The rest of the family saw it, too.

As he hung up the phone, Mr. Ladd said unbelievingly, "That was Sam. I'd left his name with the broker* in case he needed to talk to me while I was away." Sam Catlett was Tank's father and a good friend to John Ladd.

"What happened?" Mrs. Ladd asked gently.

"The newspaper deal just fell through."

"What?" his wife cried. "But I thought it was all set!"

"The present owners changed their minds." Mr. Ladd sat down in a wicker-backed chair at the small telephone table. "They decided not to sell. That was the only one we could afford. Now it's gone."

Josh asked softly, "What're you going to do, Dad?"

"I don't know, Son."

"We won't move back to the Mainland, will we?" Tiffany asked fearfully.

"I hope not!" her father said. "Especially with Josh's allergy being so much better here. But if I can't buy a newspaper pretty soon, we may have to think about it."

Josh's world seemed to explode. "Oh, no, Dad! I can't leave Tank again! I just couldn't stand to be that lonely anymore!"

Nathan let out a happy shriek. "Yea! We're going back to Los Angeles!"

"Nathan, please! Don't shout," his mother reprimanded. "I know you're not happy about living in Hawaii, but you'll get used to it."

"I'm the only one who doesn't have a best friend," the

boy protested. "I hate Hawaii!"

His mother reached out and gave him a big hug. "We'll talk about this later. Children, television cameras will be here soon. Run get cleaned up in case they want to include our family in their news story."

Josh barely heard. "You could get a job teaching school here," he pointed out to his father. "Or you could work for somebody else."

"Son, I'm going to pursue my dream of being a publisher here. If that doesn't work out, then I'll do whatever has to be done to support our family. Since it'd cost less to live in California, and I might be able to get my teaching job back, it's logical to think about that as an alternative. We'll see what happens.

"Now, excuse me, Son. I've got to call those other television stations."

Josh was normally a fast-moving, fast-talking boy, but he walked slowly into the adjacent small room that he shared with Nathan. His brother chattered away about how much he missed California, but Josh didn't listen.

He sank slowly onto the edge of his twin bed. Go back to the San Fernando Valley where he couldn't breathe because of his allergy? Go back to being rushed to the hospital emergency room when his allergy was especially bad? Worst of all, leave Tank after just getting back together? The thought almost made Josh sick.

Soon the Hilo television crew arrived, accompanied by a well-dressed young woman. She introduced herself as

Stacy Cribbs, the anchorwoman.* Answering a few of Mr. Ladd's questions about the kids who had been saved, she watched while the lights and cameras were set up.

"I just checked with the hospital, Mr. Ladd. Both kids are going to be all right. They were supposed to stay in close to shore, but their babysitter got interested in a book and took her eyes off them.

"Their father's flying out from Washington," she added. "I'm sure he'll want to meet you, Mr. Ladd.

"Well, now," she continued, "before we do anything else, let's see that video your boy shot. I brought a portable playback so we can all view it."

The video cassette was removed from the camera and snapped into a large player brought in from the station's van. The Ladd family and television people all leaned forward, watching intently while the near-drowning episode rolled on the screen.

When it was over, everyone lost interest except Josh. He frowned, remembering the man with the cold, hard eyes who had unknowingly stared right into the camera.

"Too bad you only had that little microphone mounted above the lens," Miss Cribbs noted. "The sound's kind of fuzzy, but the photography is fine."

She turned to Josh. "You seem to have a natural talent with a camera."

"I'm going to get a camera of my own pretty soon," he replied.

"Good for you! Okay, everybody, let's get this done,"

Miss Cribbs efficiently ordered. "Mr. Ladd, you and Josh follow the crew. They'll get you set up, and I'll do the on-camera interview. We've got to beat those guys from Honolulu! They'll be here on the first flight."

She was right. She had just interviewed Mr. Ladd and his son when the other television crews started phoning from the lobby. Mrs. Ladd asked them to please wait.

Miss Cribbs almost pushed Mr. and Mrs. Ladd into the bedroom Josh and Nathan shared. As the door closed, Nathan asked, "What're they doing?"

"They're negotiating for rights to use the tape," Tiffany explained.

"What's that mean?" Nathan asked.

"They're trying to buy permission to use the tape on their program."

"More than that," Josh said. "I think Miss Cribbs wants to have it shown across the country."

"But that's not theirs!" Nathan protested. "It's Josh's! He shot it. They should ask him."

"I think she'll offer to sell it to other stations for Dad and give him part of the money they pay for using it," Tiffany told Nathan.

Josh didn't care. He didn't even care that he had just been interviewed for television. He was thinking about what a terrible thing it would be if they had to move back to California and leave Tank.

His older sister seemed to be thinking about that, too. "I don't want to leave Marsha," she admitted. Marsha was

Tank's older sister, and she and Tiffany were really good friends.

The newscaster was smiling when she breezed out of the bedroom, trailed by Mr. and Mrs. Ladd. She rushed over to the videotape and picked it up. "We're too close to deadline to drive back to the studio," she announced briskly. "We'll use the van to roll* the tape interview segment I just did with father and son.

"Then we'll feed in the home video," she said, waving the tape. "There won't be time to edit it, but the producer can cut it before it goes on the air, if he's alert.

"Mr. Ladd, I appreciate you letting us show this ahead of those big city TV boys. You stay with me while we get this ready to air, then you can have your original back. Tomorrow, if you'll bring it by the station, I'll make a dupe* for network and cable releases, as we agreed."

At eleven o'clock, the Ladd family gathered around the twenty-four-inch television set in the parents' room to watch the rescue segment. The TV station had not edited the ending. For a moment after the rescue was completed, the big screen was filled with the face of the spectator in the white aloha shirt.

Josh frowned, thinking, "It sure looks like him!"

The interview Miss Cribbs had done with him and his father followed immediately, but Josh kept thinking about the mean face.

His mother said, "Why, Josh, you appear downright sad! I thought you'd enjoy being on TV."

"You're still upset about maybe having to move back to the Mainland, aren't you, Son?" Josh's father asked.

That was part of the reason, so Josh nodded but didn't answer as the news concluded.

His father snapped off the set. "Bedtime, kids! Your mother and I will pray about what to do now that the newspaper deal fell through. In the morning, we'll decide on the next step."

Tiffany yawned and stretched. "Even if you have to go back to Honolulu, Dad, I hope Mom can drive us on around to the volcanoes. Maybe we'll be lucky and one will erupt."

"That's possible," her father replied. "It happens often on this island."

"Maybe we'll find Pele, too," Nathan said sleepily.

Everyone laughed at the idea, and the kids went to bed. Josh had a hard time sleeping, but finally drifted off.

His father awakened him early. "Josh, the phone's been ringing for an hour. All the media—newspapers, radio stations, everyone—want stories. You and Nathan get dressed. Your mother and I have decided we'll all leave for the day before the news people spoil our trip."

In less than an hour, the family sat in a small restaurant overlooking the ocean as they ate a leisurely breakfast. They ordered pink guava* juice, melon-like papaya*, and toast. Rice was automatically served with every meal in Hawaiian restaurants.

When they had finished, Mr. Ladd put down his

napkin. "I'm going to phone the hospital and see how the senator's kids are. I'll be right back."

But he wasn't. After fifteen minutes of waiting, Mrs. Ladd became concerned. "Josh, please go see what's keeping your father."

There was only one telephone in an outside booth, but Josh's father wasn't there. The boy checked in the car and the restroom and even asked the Oriental waitress.

Slowly, feeling uneasy, Josh reported back to his mother, sister and brother: "I can't find Dad anyplace!"

Chapter Three

THE SEARCH BEGINS

Mary Ladd set her glass of guava juice down so hard that the silverware jumped on the table. "What do you mean—you can't find your father?"

"Just that, Mom!" Josh answered. "I've looked everywhere. The phone booth, the car, the bathroom..."

"Tiffany, you stay with your brother. I'll help Josh look again."

A few minutes later, mother and son stood outside the restaurant. Theirs was the only car in the parking lot.

Mrs. Ladd's attractive face was slightly flushed. "I just can't understand it, Josh! Where could he have gone? And why?"

Josh was a little scared but tried not to show it. "Here comes a little kid. I'll ask him; maybe he's seen Dad."

The boy was of Asian descent, about Nathan's age, with black hair and dark eyes. He came uncertainly toward Josh and Mrs. Ladd.

"You da kine* Ladd family?" he asked a little shyly.

Josh realized that the boy spoke pidgin, the mixture of

23

Hawaiian, English and other languages that the state's local people used.

"Yes," Mrs. Ladd replied, leaning over to look anxiously into the boy's face. "Did Mr. Ladd send you? Where is he?"

The local boy shrugged and handed her a note.

Mrs. Ladd grabbed it and quickly unfolded it. Josh stepped closer to read it, too.

It had been printed in block letters with a soft lead pencil. "I'll trade your husband for the tape."

There was more, but before Josh could read it, his mother clutched the note to her breast and whispered, "Oh, no! John's been kidnapped! Tape? What tape?"

She closed her eyes quickly and then opened them. "Little boy, where did you . . .? Josh, where's that boy who brought the note?"

Josh pointed. The boy was across the quiet road and running as fast as his bare feet would take him toward some plumeria* and oleanders*.

"Catch him, Josh!" his mother urgently ordered. "We've got to find out who gave him the note!"

Josh ran hard, but when he pushed through the dense growth where the boy had gone, he had disappeared. Josh ran back and forth, searching along a row of twelve-foot high bougainvillea*. He saw only a skinny yellow dog that barked at Josh from a distance. Josh ran back to his mother.

Tiffany and Nathan had joined her. She had obviously

shown them the note, for both kids ran toward Josh, calling out in their excitement.

Josh sighed. "Mom, I'm sorry, but he got away."

Mary Ladd nodded and lightly touched Josh's shoulder. "It's all right."

Glancing down at the note which she had crumpled, she muttered, "He must mean the videotape that the Hilo station aired last night. But why would anybody want it enough to kidnap John? And where *is* that tape?"

Josh motioned toward the outside phone booth. "You'd better call the police."

"No!" Mrs. Ladd spoke sharply. "The note says we mustn't call the authorities." She tapped the paper with a long, slender forefinger.

Josh glanced down and read the warning. Looking up, he asked, "What're we going to do?"

"Give them the tape, of course!" Mrs. Ladd dug in her purse. "Here! Use the spare key the rental people gave us and look in the trunk."

Josh took the key and ran to the back end of the rented sedan. His mother followed, nervously asking, "What possible value can a tape have? Why didn't John just give it to them? Oh, I just can't believe this is happening!"

The video camera was in the trunk, but there was no tape. Mrs. Ladd ordered a search inside the car, including under and behind the seats. She also had all the flight bags searched.

"Nothing!" Josh said with a shrug.

"It's probably back in our hotel room. Come on, children!" Mary Ladd rushed back inside the restaurant to pay the cashier while the rest of the family got into the car and buckled their seat belts.

Josh didn't know what to think. It was all so unexpected and unreal. He glanced at his sister and brother.

Nathan was puckering his face as though he was about to cry.

Tiffany became the brave big sister, comforting the little boy, but with a quiver in her voice: "Don't worry; Dad will be fine."

Their mother ran out, slid behind the wheel and drove as fast as she dared back to the hotel. She whipped into the underground garage.

Josh jogged ahead with the room key his mother had given him. But as he started to insert the key in the lock, he stopped in surprise. The door wasn't locked.

"Oh! Oh!" he whispered.

Then he raised his voice. "Mom!"

Shoving open the door with his foot, he saw everything inside was a mess. Every drawer had been opened and the contents thrown on the carpet. The same was true of the closet.

"Just like when we came over to Hawaii the first time, and you got into that trouble at the Shark Pit,* Josh!" Nathan recalled.

Tiffany shook her head. "The burglar who did that's in jail! This must have been done by the people who want the video."

Josh agreed. "They probably did this right after we left. They must not have found it, because they either followed us or found us."

"How could they have found us?" Nathan asked doubtfully.

"If there were two or more, one could have followed us and seen where we stopped for breakfast. When the one who made this mess didn't find what he wanted, he could have used a car phone to call the other guy who knew where we were."

Tiffany nodded and picked up some of her parents' clothing from the floor. "Then when Dad went outside to use the phone, they were waiting. But who? Why do they want that tape?"

Josh went to his mother. She was sitting at the little table by the phone, staring at it. "Mom, you going to call the police now?"

She sighed and slowly shook her head. "I want to, but I don't dare."

"What are you going to do?" Josh asked as his sister and brother came up behind them.

"I'm so mixed up, I can't think straight! Maybe if I had Barbara Catlett here to talk it over with—"

Josh interrupted. "Yeah! Tank! Have her bring Tank!"

"And Marsha!" Tiffany exclaimed.

"Tank could help us find Dad," Josh added.

Mary Ladd squared her chin and reached for the phone,

but it rang just as she touched it. She jumped and jerked her hand back as if the phone were a snake that had almost bitten her. Letting it ring three times, she finally answered it.

"Hello?"

Josh watched as his mother listened a moment. Her eyes slowly widened, and her free hand flew to her throat.

"Who is this?" she asked, her voice unsteady. "But I don't have the tape! I don't know where. . .Twenty-four hours! But I told you. . .Hello? Hello?" She slowly put down the receiver and looked at her children.

"The kidnappers who've got Dad?" Josh guessed.

His mother nodded. "He said to get the tape and be ready to deliver it to the place he tells us when he calls back. If he doesn't have the tape by this time tomorrow—" Her voice broke, and she didn't finish.

Josh glanced at the digital clock on the nightstand by his parents' bed. It read 9:55 a.m.

"What're we going to do?" Nathan wailed.

Mary Ladd took a slow, deep breath. "First, we're going to pray. Then I'll phone the Catletts. After that, we'll see."

She stood, reached out and gathered her children inside the loving circle of her arms. Josh felt his mother tremble as she prayed.

When she had finished, she quietly asked the children to pick up the mess the burglar had made. They obeyed in silence while she called Honolulu. Josh heard her explaining the situation to Tank's mother.

When Mrs. Ladd hung up the phone, she told the children, "She'll call Sam at the store."

"What about Tank?" Josh asked.

"And Marsha?" Tiffany added.

"They were there, so she'll explain everything to them after she talks to her husband. Barbara says they'll all come over on the first available flight. Now, please finish picking up while I try to think where John might have put that tape and why someone wants it enough to take him hostage."

Josh began to feel a little better. He would have someone to talk to when Tank arrived. Maybe together they could figure out where to find Josh's father.

Suddenly Mary Ladd reached for the telephone and called the front desk. "This is Mary Ladd in room 606. Did my husband place something in your hotel safe late last night? He did? Thank you."

She hung up and hugged the three kids who came running. "After the newspeople offered to make arrangements to air that tape on national television and cable networks, your father must have thought the best place for the tape would be in the hotel safe. I'll run down and get it."

When she returned with the tape, the kids had straightened up everything.

"Well," she announced as she sat on the edge of the bed, "now we've got the tape, and I think I know why the kidnappers want it so much.

"I've been thinking," she continued while the children gathered around her. "This must have something to do with Senator DeMott's children almost drowning—"

"Of course!" Josh interrupted, "I should have thought of it before!"

"Thought of what?" his mother asked.

"I saw something when we looked at the tape."

"What? What?" his mother demanded, clutching him by both shoulders. "What did you see?"

"A man—"

"Who was he?" Mrs. Ladd interrupted.

"I...I don't know. He looked sort of familiar, but..."

"Joshua, for goodness' sake!" his mother exploded. "Your father's in danger from something that's on that tape! What did you see?"

"Mom, maybe if I ran the tape you could see for yourself."

"All right, Josh. Get the camera!" his mother excitedly ordered. "Here! Insert the tape. While we're setting up, tell me what you saw."

"Well," Josh said as he brought the camera to his mother, "it was when I put the camera down while Dad and the beach guard were coming ashore. I didn't know the camera would continue to run. I thought when I took my thumb off the button—"

"Joshua!" his mother exclaimed. "Get to the point, please."

"I'm trying to tell you! The camera kept running, so

when I put it down—"

"Yeah!" Nathan broke in. "I saw that when it ran on TV. The ground and the sky and the people looked like they were whirling around."

"Nathan, not now, please!" Mrs. Ladd's voice was a little high. "What about it, Josh?"

"Well, the people who came to watch the rescue didn't know the camera was running, either. Here, it's all set up. You can see for yourself."

The family leaned over the tiny, one-inch screen as Josh pushed the button and the playback began. While it went through the rescue segment, Josh continued his explanation.

"As I was saying, I thought I recognized one of the people who was on camera, but I just couldn't place him. But just now, when you mentioned Senator DeMott, well, I knew where I'd seen that man."

"Where?" Mrs. Ladd asked.

"On the news a month or so ago. They were having all those congressional hearings about crime bosses. One of the men Senator DeMoss was questioning was the man I saw on the video."

"Lapser?" Josh's mother asked. "Was it Leopold Lapser?"

"Yeah! That's it! You'll see him on the playback in just a second."

His mother raised both hands so her forefingers touched her temples as though she was thinking very hard.

"Lapser! I remember him. He was charged with all kinds of crimes, but he fled—became a fugitive."

She dropped her hands and impulsively hugged Josh. "Of course! Now it makes sense. Lapser must be hiding here in the islands. He was among the spectators at the beach, and when he saw himself on your tape during the news last night, he figured he had to get that tape before it ran nationally."

"Yeah!" Josh exclaimed. "If it ran again, someone would probably recognize him, and then the cops would know where to find him."

"That makes sense," Tiffany agreed. "So, now that we know why they took Dad and want this tape—Say! It's over, and I didn't see that part."

"Me either!" Josh cried in surprise. "It was there last night. Here! Let's re-run it. Fast!"

The video ran again, but there was no segment such as had aired the night before.

"It's gone!" Josh whispered. "But how?"

"The television station!" Mrs. Ladd cried. "I'll ask them."

In two minutes, Mrs. Ladd had the Hilo station on the line. "Hello! News director? My name is Mary Ladd . . ."

Josh listened anxiously while his mother talked into the receiver. She didn't say anything about her husband being kidnapped but asked about the missing segment of the tape.

"You mean," Mrs. Ladd asked slowly, "you did my

husband a favor by editing out that part after the rescue—
the part that wasn't airworthy—so he could run it on other
stations?

"I see. What happened to that part? I mean, is that like
in the movies when outtakes* end up on the cutting room
floor?"

She listened a moment and then said in a weak, tiny
voice, "Thank you."

As she hung up, she swallowed hard. Josh saw her chin
tremble.

"What is it, Mom?" he asked anxiously.

"Editing of videotape is done electronically. Anything
they don't want is destroyed without a trace. Something
about little molecules being rearranged magnetically."

Nathan clapped his hands. "Good! Then the tape is
gone, and the guys who've got Dad won't care anymore."

"Wrong!" Tiffany exclaimed impatiently. "That means
we can't give the tape to the man, even if we wanted to,
because the part he wants is gone forever."

"Worse than that, children," their mother explained.
"The kidnapper—Mr. Lapser or whoever he is—will
think we cheated him and still have the part he wants."

Josh licked his lips, feeling his mouth suddenly go dry.
"If he finds that out. . ." Josh began and almost added,
"Then we'll never seen Dad again!" But he checked
himself.

"He mustn't find out," Mrs. Ladd said firmly. "Not
until after we've got your father back."

"How're you going to do that?" Nathan asked, his eyes wide, as though he realized what Josh had almost said.

"We'll find a way," his mother assured him. "Now, let's try to think while we're waiting for the Catletts."

In the two hours it took for the Catletts to arrive, the Ladd family worked out a plan. Feeling hopeful, Mrs. Ladd drove with Josh to the airport.

Barbara Catlett was first off the plane, followed by her husband, Sam, their daughter, Marsha, and their son, Tank. Josh was surprised to also see his friend Roger Okamoto getting off.

"Now," Josh thought as he rushed forward to greet his buddies, "we have to find Dad before it's too late!"

Chapter Four

THE VOLCANO ERUPTS

Josh had expected six people to ride back from the airport, but Roger's surprise arrival made it a snug fit in the midsize sedan. Mrs. Ladd asked Sam Catlett to drive.

"I'm really anxious to get back to the hotel," she admitted. "I left Tiffany to answer the phone in case the kidnappers called."

During the short drive, the Catletts and Roger Okamoto listened in silence as Josh's mother told everything that had happened, ending with the deadline to exchange the videotape for her husband.

Josh saw Tank's father glance at his watch. Sam Catlett was a slender, wiry man in his late thirties who dressed in the finest suits his chain store carried. His blond hair was perfectly styled.

"Less than twenty-two hours," he said softly. Then he raised his gray eyes to watch the roadway again. "We've got to think of something to help get John back."

Various proposals were offered. Finally, Mr. Catlett

came up with a suggestion which the others thought was worth a try.

"Then we're agreed?" Sam asked. When he heard the murmured yeses, he said, "Now, Mary, let's go over everything again so we all understand what needs to be done."

As they finalized their plans, they neared the hotel. Josh saw that the parking lot was full of television panel trucks.

"Oh, oh!" he exclaimed, pointing. "They've probably come to interview Dad about the rescue and to get the tape. That's something we hadn't planned on. Now what'll we do?"

Before anyone could answer, Mrs. Catlett cried, "Look! They're all running from the hotel to their trucks! They must have seen us coming."

"No," Tank said. "It's something else." Tank had straight blond hair bleached almost white from the sun. He was slightly taller than Josh and weighed a bit more. Like Josh, Tank's arms and shoulders were unusually strong from all the swimming he did.

From the front seat, Mrs. Ladd whispered, "Oh, I hope it's not bad news about John!"

Sam snapped on the car radio. "Let's see if we can find an all-news station."

In a moment, he found part of a news bulletin. "The volcanic eruption, reported about ten minutes ago, is sending two flows of lava running along a rift toward Pake*, a sleepy, former fishing village on the Big Island."

"A volcano's erupting on this island?" Josh exclaimed. "Can we see it from here?"

Tank answered in his usual slow, deliberate way that was the exact opposite of Josh's rushed sentences. "I doubt it. Kilauea* is the one that's always blowing up. But we can't see it because that old mountain to our left blocks the view."

From his position at the left rear window, Tank ducked low, looking to his left. "Nope! Can't see anything."

Mrs. Ladd anxiously shut her eyes. "Oh, Lord! That's all we need right now. A volcanic eruption!"

"At least it'll keep the press away from us and from trying to interview Dad," Josh pointed out, leaning forward from the back seat to pat his mother lightly on the shoulder.

"Volcano Observatory spokespeople say," the radio announcer continued, "that if the seventy-foot-high fiery fountains keep pumping lava at the present rate, the flow along the east flank of Kilauea may force evacuation of Pake's three hundred occupants. However, evacuation is not now planned."

"See?" Tank exclaimed. "It *is* Kilauea!"

"Shhh!" his sister ordered. "I want to hear this."

Josh's head soon reeled from the statistics the announcer provided as background. "In 1960, the eruption lasted thirty-seven days and destroyed two villages, including seventy-eight buildings. More than three square miles of countryside were covered before the river of lava reached the sea. Nearly five hundred acres were added to the shoreline."

"Boy," Josh exclaimed, "can you imagine what that would be like to photograph?"

Mrs. Ladd turned wordlessly and looked at her son. Instantly, he lowered his eyes, sorry he had thought of his own interests when his father was in danger.

The announcer continued to give eruption statistics from past volcanic activity while he waited for the latest word from observers near the mountain. "A maximum temperature of 2,150 degrees was measured in an eruption at Kilauea-Iki.* One eruption produced more than one hundred-eleven million cubic yards of lava.

"Another eruption created a fiery fountain that measured one thousand-seven hundred feet high, although some claimed the fountain hit nearly two thousand feet."

"Wow!" Tank exclaimed. "That's more than a quarter of a mile straight up!"

Mrs. Ladd reached over and turned the radio volume down. "I just hope John's not in any danger from that volcano," she said quietly.

Sam eased the sedan into the hotel's underground parking lot. "Not likely, Mary. Well, let's get upstairs and see if Tiffany's heard from those people again. Don't forget what you have to say."

As they got out of the elevator on the sixth floor, Josh turned to Roger. "You haven't said one word since we picked you up. You okay?" He looked closely at the slender thirteen-year-old with pale brown skin and black hair that stuck out over his ears.

"Haven't you noticed?" Tank asked. "Roger's bashful around girls and grown-ups."

"What have you been thinking, Roger?" Josh probed.

"I was thinking," Roger responded, "that Pele is plenty huhu.*"

Josh almost laughed at Roger's notion that a goddess could cause a volcano to erupt because she was angry. But a glance at Roger's face showed he wasn't joking.

"You believe in the legend of fire?" Josh asked instead.

"A little." Roger thought a moment and then added, "More than a little. My grandfather saw her once, and lots of people have seen her." Even though he could speak perfect English, Roger's sentences had a tendency to go up at the end, almost as if he were asking a question.

Josh couldn't believe what he was hearing. A modern, intelligent person believing in a fire goddess. "Your grandfather saw Pele?"

"Yes."

Tank reached out and touched Josh and Roger's arms, slowing them down. The three boys fell behind the adults. "What's she like—this Pele?" Tank asked.

"Some people say she's beautiful; others say she's like an ugly old witch."

Josh couldn't help asking, "What'd your grandfather say she looked like?"

"Tell you later," Roger promised as they neared the

room.

When Mrs. Ladd's key opened the hotel door, Tiffany rushed to meet her, trailed by Nathan. Both of them were excitedly talking at once.

"Mom!" Tiffany cried. "The kidnapper called again! I told him you'd gone out for something. He's going to call back any minute."

"Yeah!" Nathan added, his eyes bright. "I thought you weren't going to get back in time."

The phone rang, and nine people spun to face it as though it were a ticking bomb.

Josh licked his lips, wondering if the plan would work.

His mother turned quickly, her eyes sweeping her family and the Catletts. "I'm not sure I can do this."

"Yes, you can!" everyone exclaimed.

Barbara Catlett pointed out, "For John's sake, you can."

Mrs. Ladd managed a weak smile. "Well, then, here goes! Pray I handle this right."

She hurried to the phone while Tiffany and Marsha gave each other a hug of greeting and comfort.

Josh joined the others as Mrs. Ladd took a deep breath and picked up the phone. She listened a moment and then, covering the receiver with her hand, announced, "It's the same voice."

"Go for it, Mom!" Josh whispered. "You can do it!"

She nodded and uncovered the receiver. "Yes, this is Mrs. Ladd. Who is this?"

There was a pause, then she said firmly, "Look, if you

won't identify yourself, how do I know this isn't some kind of a cruel joke? If you've got my husband, put him on the line. Otherwise, I'm going to hang up!"

Josh took a slow, deep breath, thinking, "Easy, Mom! Easy!" The plan had sounded good as they discussed it in the car, but now it seemed too risky.

Nobody breathed while Mrs. Ladd listened to the man's response. Then she lowered her voice and spoke firmly. "Naturally I want my husband back, but I want to be sure you're really holding him before I talk about the tape. Put him on the line now or. . ."

She paused while Josh and the other eight people in the room anxiously leaned forward. Mrs. Ladd seemed aware of their support. She tipped the receiver slightly away from her ear so the caller's voice could be heard.

Josh caught the faint words. "He's not with me right now. I'm at a public phone. But I assure you, lady—"

"Call me back when he can talk. When I hear his voice and know he's all right, then we'll discuss the tape. Good-bye!"

"Wait!" The word came sharply over the phone so Josh and the others heard it. "You win this one, lady. I'll call you back in half an hour so your husband can say something. But you'd better not be playing games with me, you hear?"

The phone clicked dead. Slowly, Mrs. Ladd lowered the receiver to the cradle. Then she sank onto the bed, her hands covering her face.

Josh glanced at the alarm clock on his parents' bedside stand. Twenty-one hours left.

"It's okay, Mom." Josh comforted his mother, putting his arm around her neck. "You did great!"

She raised her face, her eyes shining and tears sliding down her cheeks. "You really think so?"

"Yes!" It was a chorus from everyone.

"Then I'd better get a hold of my emotions," Mrs. Ladd said, standing and straightening her shoulders. "I've got to sound brave for John's sake when he comes on the line."

"Mom, you're the bravest," Nathan said gravely, clutching her about the waist.

"The bravest!" Barbara Catlett agreed with a teary smile.

"Thank you," Mrs. Ladd said softly. "If it weren't for the support you're giving me, I'm not sure I could go through with this."

"I'd better get that other car rented fast," Tank's father announced, picking up the phone. "I hope it's ready by the time that guy calls back."

"All set," he said after arranging to have the car delivered to the hotel. "Now we're ready."

"Not quite!" Josh suddenly cried. "I almost forgot to get a cassette for Dad's camera."

"Be sure it's a new one," his mother ordered, waving her hands quickly to urge him to action.

"Don't worry!" the boy assured her, dashing to the closet where he had placed several unused cassettes when straightening up after the place had been ransacked.

Tank followed him to the closet door. "You're not going to try taking pictures of him when he meets your mother?"

"Sure am! I'll use the telephoto lens." Josh checked the cassette. It was still in the plastic wrap, fresh from the manufacturer.

"Isn't that a terrible risk?"

Josh nodded soberly. "But not as terrible as what Dad's taking, or Mom's going to."

"I see what you mean," Tank said after a moment.

Conversation died down. Josh thought so much needed to be talked about, but nobody seemed to want to; not even the usually gabby Tiffany and Marsha.

A half hour passed. Forty-five minutes. Josh began fighting fear. Maybe Mom had overdone it. Maybe the man wasn't going to call back. Maybe. . .maybe that was because John Ladd *couldn't* come to the phone.

It rang so suddenly that everyone jumped. Josh's mouth went dry with fear as he took a couple of quick steps to be near his mother when she answered.

"Pray for wisdom," she whispered, and picked up the phone. She held the receiver away from her ear so those crowding quietly around her could hear. "Hello?"

"Here's your husband." Josh recognized the same voice. He swallowed hard and strained to hear. After a moment's silence, his father's familiar voice came over the phone. "Mary?"

"Oh, John! Thank God! Are you all right?"

"I'm fine."

Josh thought his father was trying hard to control his voice. Probably so he wouldn't worry his wife and family.

"Keep talking, John," Mary said eagerly. "I want to hear your voice; to know it's really you and that you're really all right!"

"I'm fine, Mary. They want the tape enough to kidnap me, but I don't think they're going to hurt me so—"

"That's enough!" The captor's voice was harsh. Josh heard sounds as though the phone was being forcibly taken from his father. "Now, lady, you satisfied?"

Mrs. Ladd took a slow breath before answering. "I'm satisfied that was my husband, yes. When will you release him?"

"You'll get him back after I get the tape. You ready to deal?"

Josh saw his mother take a few more quick, short breaths to keep her voice even before she answered. The boy knew she was walking a fine line, negotiating to give up a tape that no longer had the portion the man wanted.

"I have the tape my son took at the beach," Mrs. Ladd said, controlling her quivering voice. "You'll get it when I see my husband walk safely into my arms."

"Look, lady! You're in no position to be telling me—"

"No, you look, mister! Kidnapping is a federal offense. The FBI will be after you if anything happens to my husband. Your only chance is to keep him alive and well! Now, is that clear?"

The man's voice was almost a growl. "What's clear is that I get that tape by the deadline, or—"

Mrs. Ladd broke in so he couldn't complete the sentence. "Very well! I'll meet you someplace where people are around so you can't pull any tricks."

"Lady, I'll choose the place."

"No, I will. Be quiet and listen! I'll meet you at the City of Refuge National Historical Park, by the Great Wall. How soon can you get there?"

"Lady, I don't like that place—"

"I said, how soon can you get there?"

"Give me two hours. Come alone!"

"No, I'll bring a friend."

The voice changed. It became soft but firm. "Then you'll never see your husband again."

Josh's mother was prepared. "And you'll never see the tape, plus the FBI will be after you at once."

There was a moment's hesitation. "Okay, lady, let's compromise. You bring one of your kids; that's all. Nobody better follow you, either."

"One of my children. Two hours," Mrs. Ladd agreed and then hung up.

Everyone gathered around her. Tank's mother slipped her arms around Josh's mother, whose body was shaking with silent sobs.

"Nobody should make my mother cry!" Josh thought fiercely. He felt angry tears form in his eyes. Glancing at Tank and Roger, he clenched his fists and determined that the three of them would somehow catch the man who had kidnapped his father and made his mother cry.

Mrs. Ladd sniffed and raised her head. She shook her dark hair out of her eyes and managed a weak smile. "So far, so good! Now, if you're all ready to play tourists, let's get started for the park."

Chapter Five

THE SPY IN THE SKY

Tank's father, Josh, Tank and Roger got out of the elevator at the lobby while the rest of the group rode down to the garage to get the Ladds' car.

"Everyone must have gone to see the volcano," Mr. Catlett observed as they walked through the deserted lobby. "Hawaii's the only place tourists run to an eruption instead of away from it."

A silver sedan pulled to the curb, followed by a van with a car rental sign painted on the side. "That's probably for me," Mr. Catlett said.

As they walked outside, Josh was surprised that the trade winds weren't blowing. In the few weeks he had lived in Hawaii, this was the first time the warm, strong breezes hadn't caressed his face when he stepped into the open. Instead, the air was quiet with a stillness that seemed strange and a little scary.

"Storm coming," Roger said knowingly, looking at the sky.

Somehow, the change in atmosphere gave Josh an

uneasy feeling. He looked at the sky. The usual clear blue bowl was gone. Instead, giant clouds rolled ponderously by, threatening the earth and burying the land with ominous black shadows.

Tank's father signed some papers offered by the van driver, who pulled away with the sedan driver.

"Get in, boys!" Mr. Catlett said. "The ladies and Nathan are just coming out of the side street."

Josh, Tank and Roger got into the back seat, just like the plan called for. All three boys were quiet as Mr. Catlett took a minute to acquaint himself with the car's instrument panel, gear system and hand brake. He eased the vehicle away from the hotel's loading zone.

Josh saw the first raindrops make little cat tracks on the windshield. The water in the bay was rough, and big swells surged toward a seawall that ran right up against the city street.

As the silver sedan eased into traffic a block behind the black car Josh's mother was driving, the rain came down harder. The swells from the open bay rushed toward the seawall, hit hard and exploded into the air. Big, white drops of water were thrown high above the street, then fell heavily on the sedan. It was as though the ocean were trying to stop them from making the trip to the City of Refuge.

Josh didn't like the feeling at all. He glanced at Tank on his left and Roger on his right. Neither boy spoke. Perhaps, Josh thought, they felt the same way.

They passed a church which Josh's father had explained to the family was the oldest on the islands. The first company of missionaries finished it in 1837, and it was still in use.

Tank's father raised his eyes to the rear view mirror. "You should go to ohana* some weeknight in that church, Josh."

"What's that?"

"Family devotions; vespers."

Josh frowned, thinking. He knew vespers was some sort of religious service, but the church where his family had been members in California didn't use the word. Their pastor wore a suit in the pulpit, but when the Ladds had gone to church with the Catletts in Honolulu, the pastor had worn robes.

"What's vespers?" Josh asked.

"It's a late afternoon or evening religious service," Mr. Catlett answered as he kept his eyes on Josh's mother's car, about a quarter of a mile ahead. "You'd enjoy it. Vespers at this church was one of the most memorable our family ever attended. Wasn't it, Tank?"

"It was different," Tank agreed. "Afterward, the choir went across to the hotel and played hymns on some kind of bamboo things."

Roger said nothing. From Tank, Josh had learned that Roger was a Buddhist*, although he had never said one word about it to Josh.

Josh's mind jumped to what lay ahead that afternoon

and whether his part would endanger his parents. "Maybe my family will go there after we get Dad back," was all he said.

They drove in silence through the rest of the town. Josh caught sight of a monkey pod tree* and others he had come to recognize. Suddenly, he thought of something.

"Oh, Mr. Catlett! The camera! It's still in Mom's car!" He held up the cassette. "I was so excited I forgot to get the camera for this."

Tank's father glanced at the boy in the rear view mirror. "I don't want to stop your mother in case somebody's watching her, but we've got to have that camera! Tell you what: we'll drive awhile and make sure nobody's following us. If it's okay, I'll catch up to her and signal her to stop."

Josh nodded and watched anxiously through the rear window as Mr. Catlett guided the car along. The road turned inland, away from the sea. It ran along through junglelike growths while the Pacific glistened in the distance.

"What do you think?" Mr. Catlett asked at length. "That the same car that's been behind us for a while?"

"No," Josh answered. "I don't think so." He turned to Tank and Roger. "Right?"

They had been watching, too. "Let's give it another five minutes and see," Tank suggested.

"I'd slow down," Mr. Catlett said, "but your mother must be anxious, Josh. She's moving right along."

A car behind them stayed well back. It didn't seem to gain or lose distance. Was it following them?

Josh began to be concerned. He had to have that camera from his mother's car before they reached the City of Refuge. Yet, if somebody was following to make sure that Mrs. Ladd was alone, it wouldn't do to be seen.

"How could I have done a dumb thing like forgetting the camera?" he whispered to Tank. "I should have gotten it when your father's car arrived."

"Old age forgetfulness, I guess." His best friend grinned.

"You're the same age I am!" Josh said, giving Tank a playful shove.

Roger had been staring out the back window. "That car has turned off."

Mr. Catlett's eyes flashed to the rear view mirror. "He sure did! Watch to see that none comes back on. Sometimes they switch cars like that when following someone."

All three boys watched. The road wound up through the jungle, but it remained empty.

"All right," Mr. Catlett announced, speeding up a little. "Josh, I'll pull up behind your mother and flash my lights when I see a place where we can pull both cars over. Get ready to jump out and get that camera. It's raining a little harder, so don't slip!"

Josh nodded, watching the windshield wipers moving rhythmically back and forth. Both cars passed through a small town of weathered wooden buildings with white ginger blooming in some yards. At the edge of town, the road stretched ahead while the jungle stood back from the highway.

"Now!" Mr. Catlett reached for his lights and pulled up fast behind the black sedan. "When we both stop, move fast, Josh! Get the camera and tell her to drive on. It's important that nobody see us together. Got that?"

"Got it!"

As Josh dashed up to the driver's side, Mrs. Ladd's face showed alarm. Raindrops hit him in the face. "Mom! I forgot the camera!"

"It's in the trunk. Here! You'll need the keys. Don't forget the telephoto lens, Josh!"

"I won't!"

It took only a minute for Josh to get the camera and telephoto lens. He slammed the trunk lid down and ran to the window to hand the keys back to his mother. He repeated Mr. Catlett's warning to her.

As Josh sprinted through the light rain back to the silver sedan, he glanced up at a sudden noise overhead.

"Uh, oh!"

A small black helicopter seemed to swoop from nowhere. Appearing above the junglelike growths, it slowed momentarily directly overhead, then zipped out of sight behind the hills.

Josh was panting and scared when he jumped into the back seat. "Did you see that?" he asked breathlessly.

"We saw it," Mr. Catlett answered quietly. "Let's hope it was just a coincidence."

Josh turned anxiously, staring into the sky. There was no sign of the helicopter, and no car followed. Still, the boy couldn't shake the feeling that something had gone wrong.

Mr. Catlett let the other car pull well ahead of him. Suddenly, he smacked the palm of his hand down hard on the steering wheel.

Josh was alarmed. "What happened?"

"I wasn't thinking! As long as we were stopped, I should have had everyone except Nathan transfer to this car."

"That's okay," Josh assured Mr. Catlett. "They're going to get out and wait for us to pick them up just before we get to the park."

"I know! But those plans were made before the rain. Oh, well. Too late now."

It was a little thing, but it made Josh squirm uneasily. He felt a shiver start along his neck and skid down his shoulders and arms, but he fought off the uncomfortable feeling.

To change the subject, he turned to Roger. "Hey! You grew up in this state. Aren't we somewhere near where a bunch of historical things happened?"

Roger looked out the window for a minute. "Yeah! Pretty soon we'll come to the Captain Cook monument. That's where the first white man to come to these islands was killed by the natives when they found out he wasn't a god they'd been expecting."

Josh nodded, remembering his father had told him about the English explorer. Not that Josh was really interested in history right now, but he didn't want to think about what the helicopter meant, or what might happen to his father.

"We're getting close to an ancient battleground," Roger continued. "Then the City of Refuge at Honaunau*."

Josh knew about that. His father had prepared them for their planned visit there. Ancient Hawaiian lawbreakers could flee for safety to certain towns, like the cities of refuge in the Old Testament. This particular city was on a shelf of lava about twenty acres in size right against the sea. It had a Great Wall on one side, with two sides facing the Pacific.

"The wall is where Mom is supposed to meet Dad's kidnapper," Josh said, thinking aloud.

"Which end?" Roger asked.

Josh blinked. "Which end?"

"Sure! It's seventeen feet wide, ten feet high and a thousand feet long."

"That's about a fifth of a mile!" Tank exclaimed. "I sure hope your mother can find that guy."

"Is there a parking lot?" Josh asked anxiously.

Roger nodded. "Lots of lava from an old flow goes right down to the parking lot."

"That's where she'll be, then." Josh was sure. "She

wants to be where people are so the kidnapper can't play any tricks."

"Strange place for a hostage exchange," Mr. Catlett mused. "The park is one of the prettiest spots in all Hawaii. Oh, I see Mary's let out Barbara, Marsha and Nathan. She must have decided to have Tiffany stay with her rather than Nathan. Make room, boys!"

Mrs. Catlett and Marsha jumped into the front seat while Josh's little brother slipped into the back.

"Did you see that helicopter?" Tank's mother asked as she buckled her seat belt.

Everyone agreed they had seen it.

"Tiffany and I think it was a spy plane!" Nathan blurted out. "They know both cars are together, and they'll use rockets on both of us when we stop to pick up Dad!"

"Nathan!" Josh exclaimed. "Don't say things like that!"

"Mary and I think it was a coincidence," Mrs. Catlett assured Josh. "That it has no bearing on us at all."

"Well," Josh said, swallowing hard, "we'll soon find out."

In a few minutes, Mr. Catlett turned the car off the highway and drove down through old, black volcanic flows toward the ocean. Josh could see a small, shallow bay, white sand beach, palm trees and the ocean beyond.

"Josh, get your camera ready. We're going to all act like tourists so the kidnappers don't get suspicious," Mr. Catlett said.

Tank snorted and almost laughed. "Won't it look funny

even for a tourist to walk around in the rain with a video camera?"

Usually quiet Roger seemed to sense that Josh was concerned. He leaned over and whispered: "Everybody knows you Mainland haoles* are pupule*. Go ahead and carry your camera, Josh. Nobody'll think anything about it."

Mr. Catlett spoke abruptly. "All right, everybody! Let's get serious. In the next few minutes, we'll either have John back safely, or. . ."

He didn't finish, but Josh knew what he meant.

The historical park was as pretty a place as Josh had ever seen. The black lava flow had come down from the mountains and poured into the sea. Now the hardened lava was lumpy and irregularly shaped. Where it ended, white sand began. Even through the rain, he could see the graceful palm trees that stood in a kind of oasis beside the Great Wall.

Josh, with camera in hand, began to move toward an outrigger canoe pulled up on the beach near the stormy, dark blue water. Tank and Roger trailed him, walking slowly and trying to appear like tourists. Mr. Catlett had taken off his coat and tie, but he still looked suspiciously like a businessman to Josh.

In the distance, he saw his mother and Tiffany approach the near end of the great wall. A man in tan shorts, blue and white aloha shirt and a pandanus* hat walked up to them.

"Hey, you guys!" Josh whispered, turning to Tank and Roger. "I think Mom's made contact with the kidnapper! I've got to get close enough to be sure I get good pictures."

"Don't make him suspicious," Tank warned.

"I won't." Josh started to move forward across the sand and through the palm trees. His heart was beating so fast he could barely breathe.

Chapter Six

THE LEGEND AND THE DANGER

It was hard to act like a tourist shooting a video in the light rain. Josh eased toward his mother, sister and the stranger, wondering where his father was. The kidnappers probably hadn't brought him too close, just as Mrs. Ladd hadn't carried the video cassette with her. That way the kidnappers couldn't grab it and run, leaving her with nothing while her husband was still a hostage.

Josh raised the video camera to his eye and began to shoot a carved wooden figure. He moved the camera slightly so that his mother, sister and the stranger were also in the viewfinder.

From behind him, Tank asked softly, "Is that the guy?"

Josh was concentrating so hard he jumped. He had forgotten his friends were with him. "I don't think it's the same one. Probably a go-between, sent to make sure Mom's got the cassette."

Josh moved on, closer to the shallow water in the bay. Small whitecaps formed on the tops of the rough, black waves, while a fine spray drifted through the air and mixed with the light rain.

"Why aren't you using the telephoto lens, Josh?" Roger asked quietly.

Josh jerked the camera from his eye and glanced down in surprise. "I forgot! Too excited, I guess."

Quickly he reached into the tubular carrying case and eased the long lens out.

"Hey," Tank whispered, "the guy's leaving!"

Josh glanced up, the telephoto lens in his hand. It was true. The man was moving down toward the far end of the Great Wall.

"Boy," Josh exclaimed, "I'll bet he's a tourist who stopped to ask Mom something!"

"Let's hope he didn't scare the real kidnapper off," Roger said.

"Yeah," Josh agreed, finishing the lens transfer. "If they're watching, they might have thought Mom met a cop or an FBI agent or someone like that."

"I don't think so," Roger mused. "They'd figure she wouldn't do anything as obvious as that."

"Let's hope you're right!" Josh slid the regular lens into the case and stood up. "Okay, look like tourists, you guys."

Twenty minutes or so passed. In the distance, Mrs. Ladd and Tiffany continued to walk along the front of the Great Wall. Nobody came near them. The rain had driven the tourists back to their cars except for a handful of teenagers.

Josh felt a little foolish as he continued to lift the video camera to his eye from time to time. He wasn't really seeing anything anymore, and he wasn't taking footage. He was becoming anxious, wondering if the people who held his father were going to show up.

"The helicopter. I'll bet it was sent to watch us and saw Mom's car was being followed." Josh spoke his thoughts aloud to Tank and Roger, who were sauntering along beside him.

"You think they won't show up?" Tank asked.

"It's beginning to look that way," Josh said with regret, feeling his stomach twist and turn.

In an hour, the three boys had seen everything in the park, or at least pretended to see it. Josh's mother and sister had ventured slightly away from the wall, but close enough that anyone looking for them could see them.

Another half hour dragged by. Josh sat on the sand by the outrigger canoe with Tank and Roger on either side. "They're not coming." He barely whispered the thought, knowing what it meant.

Glancing toward the Great Wall, he saw his mother and sister moving slowly back toward the parking lot. Their shoulders were slumped.

"They're giving up!" he exclaimed.

"It's been almost two hours," Tank said softly.

"Something went wrong!" Josh fiercely squeezed out. "Let's get back to the car. We're no closer to getting Dad back, and the twenty-four-hour deadline is passing fast!

But maybe the kidnappers will call when we get to the hotel."

Everyone sat gloomily in the hotel room staring at the telephone. It did not ring. Everything had been discussed. The plan had gone wrong. Maybe the helicopter pilot had warned the kidnappers. Maybe they had seen the tourist sharing his impressions about the City of Refuge with Mrs. Ladd and Tiffany and thought the man was an FBI agent. Maybe the kidnappers had changed their minds and weren't going to exchange John Ladd for the video after all.

A new plan was needed, but that couldn't be worked out until it was known if the kidnappers would ever phone again.

Josh was scared, thinking about what could happen, yet knowing there was absolutely nothing anybody could do until the kidnappers called. *If* they called again.

To get his mind off the terrible thoughts racing through his brain, Josh turned on the television set.

"Josh, if you watch TV, you need to keep the volume down, just in case the phone rings," his mother said. She was sitting with her head bowed. Josh was sure she was praying.

He sprawled on his stomach in front of the set with Tank and Roger and watched the continuing eruption of Kilauea. It was spectacular; Josh had never seen anything like it.

The news helicopter taking the footage occasionally

caught a flash of other aircraft. The sky seemed full of chartered planes flying tourists over to see what the announcer called "the drive-in volcano."

"Look at that!" Josh exclaimed, keeping his voice low. "A whole river of melted rock flowing down the mountain toward the sea!"

The lava was a strange, red-hot mixture topped with a sort of black crust. It moved like a living thing, a giant snake that twisted and turned, inching itself across the ground, devouring everything before it.

Tank lay on his back, propping himself up on his elbows. "It's still heading for that little village. See? The news helicopter is passing over it now."

Josh saw a small cluster of buildings in the foreground, planted fields beyond that and, way in the background, smoke a quarter-mile wide from the river of lava.

"I'm sure glad none of us lives in that place!" Roger said. "If the lava keeps coming, it'll bury that town fifty feet deep."

Josh rolled over to look at Roger. "Fifty feet deep? You kidding me?"

"Happened before," Roger assured him.

The television station switched from the sky camera to a ground crew stationed between the village and the volcano. As the boys watched, five coco palms swayed in the wind caused by the intense heat of the approaching flow. The lava inched forward, perhaps four feet high. Some brush at the bottom of the trees exploded. Flames climbed the slender palm trunks and touched the leafy fronds at the top. They writhed and twisted. Shortly afterward, only the blackened partial trunks remained, ghostly white, like bones standing upright.

"It's scary!" Josh breathed.

Roger sat cross-legged, as he often did. "Now maybe you can understand why so many locals believe in the legend of Pele."

"You were going to tell us about your grandfather meeting her—this legendary fire goddess."

Roger opened his mouth just as the telephone rang.

Everybody's head swiveled toward it. Josh leaped up and stood trembling. The volcano, the legends and all else were forgotten.

Mrs. Ladd had been lying down on the bed, but she jumped up and reached for the phone in a single movement.

"Easy!" Tank's father cautioned her. He got up from where he had been sitting in a rattan chair staring out the window at the ocean. "Remember, you've still got the tape they want."

"Yeah, Mom!" Josh added, standing by her side. "Be cool!"

Everyone circled Mrs. Ladd as she picked up the phone on the third ring. She held it slightly away from her right ear so that the others could hear.

"Hello."

"Mary Ladd?" The man's voice sounded different to

Josh from the one who had called before.

"Yes. Who's this?"

"Senator DeMott. Your husband helped save my children's lives. I just flew in from Washington and wanted to thank him..."

Josh didn't hear the rest. Apparently no one else did either. There were so many sighs that Josh realized everyone, including himself, had stopped breathing for a minute.

Josh's mother was having a hard time talking. He guessed she had been disappointed, expecting the kidnappers to call. She pressed the receiver to her ear. Josh and the others drifted away, their interest absorbed by the more important matter at hand.

"Senator, I deeply appreciate your call," Mrs. Ladd said, her voice shaking, "but it's not necessary for you to come see my husband..."

Josh spun around. "He wants to come see Dad?"

His mother cupped the phone quickly with her hand and whispered fiercely, "Shh!"

Everyone crowded around again, watching Mrs. Ladd as she dealt with this unexpected problem. "No," she said into the phone, "he's not here right now. I'm sorry, I don't know when to expect him...No, please! Don't trouble yourself. Don't feel you must come over and...Yes, I can understand that when you've just seen your children in the hospital and realize they'd be drowned if it hadn't been for...No, please! Don't take your valuable time to drop by on your way to the airport!"

Josh saw his mother's eyes were wide and her hands were shaking. "Well, my husband may not be back by then, but if you insist, I'll meet you for a moment in the lobby...All right, within the hour."

She hung up the phone slowly and turned with a stricken look on her face. "Now I can understand why he's so effective in Congress. He's persistent! I couldn't stop him from coming by."

"What'll you do when he asks about Dad?" Josh questioned.

"Well, I'll have to think about that before he gets here. Obviously, I can't tell him that John's being held hostage..."

The phone's sharp ring rattled everyone. Josh saw the panicked look on his mother's face as she reached for the phone. Again, she held it away from her ear so the others could hear.

"You didn't play by the rules, lady!"

Josh recognized the voice. It had an angry tone.

"What...what do you mean?" Mrs. Ladd asked, reaching up with her free hand to grip her other hand.

Josh realized his mother was shaking hard. He felt sorry for her and angry with the man who was making her so upset.

"Don't play dumb with me, lady! Our chopper pilot spotted the car you had following you! You're lucky we're even calling."

"I . . . I'm sorry." Mrs. Ladd's voice was low but steady. "I was going to give you the tape."

"We'll try once more," the voice interrupted. "But this time, no tricks. You follow orders, or we'll put your husband where he'll never be found! Got that?"

"Y-yes."

"Good! Now, here's what you do. . ."

Josh's mother repeated the instructions aloud and then hung up the phone. A look of renewed hope shone on her face. "This time it's got to go right." She hurried to the bed and snatched up her purse. "I hope I can find that place."

Josh grabbed at her arm. "Mom! The senator's on his way over here right now!"

Mrs. Ladd straightened up, clutching her purse. "Oh, I forgot! Well, my husband's more important. I've got to leave now to meet the men who are holding him."

"I'll follow you, Mary," Tank's father offered.

"No!" Her voice was firm. "You heard him. If I don't obey his rules. . ."

"But you can't risk going off by yourself!" Tank's mother protested. "What if they grab you, too?"

"They don't want me," Josh's mother said with conviction. "They just want this tape, and I just want my husband back. I've got to go alone."

Josh followed his mother as she headed for the door. "Mom, you can't!"

"I have no choice, Josh!" She turned and swept him

up into her arms. "Please try to understand." She motioned for Tiffany and Nathan to come into her arms with Josh.

For a long moment, she held them silently. Josh felt her body trembling. Then he heard her speak softly. He stole a quick glance upward. She was praying.

Releasing her children, she looked across at Sam and Barbara. "Please take care of them until I get back—with their father."

Then she was gone.

Josh stood in stunned silence, looking at Tank and Roger. It had all happened so fast...

His thought was broken off by another, more alarming one. "The tape! Suppose those men don't just take her word for it? Suppose they bring a playback unit and look at the video before they let Dad go?"

Tank's father cleared his throat. It was a nervous habit Josh had noticed Mr. Catlett had. "Your mother, Barbara and I had discussed that possibility earlier. Mary has completely rewound the tape, so if they do view it, they'll see it from the beginning.

"Because they're in a hurry, they almost surely won't stay long enough to see it through to the end."

"But what if they do?" Josh protested. "The whole thing only takes a couple of minutes. Suppose they fast-forward it or run it through to make sure that it's all there? They're liable to hurt Mom!"

Tank's mother reached over and gently touched Josh

on both shoulders. "They won't hurt her. She'll be all right."

Josh turned in fear toward his older sister. Sometimes she was bossy and tended to take charge, but today she seemed unsure of herself. She stood, tears glistening in the corners of her eyes.

Josh glanced down at his little brother. Nathan might be small, but he was not little inside. He raised his voice. "They won't hurt her because we won't let them, will we, Josh?"

Josh realized Nathan had no idea how helpless he really was, how helpless they all were. Unless...

Josh glanced up at Mr. Catlett. "We can't follow Mom, but maybe we could take a shortcut and get there ahead of her!"

"I don't know if there is a shortcut," Tank's father said as he frowned. "And even if there is, I'm not sure what good it would do to rush there ahead of her."

"She has to stop for gas. She mentioned that a while ago, but your car's almost full. We can beat her! We'd be there so we could watch." Josh was fighting to keep his fear from making his voice crack. "We could be witnesses. Maybe nobody else'll be there, but if we are, then they won't hurt Mom. Not with people watching!"

"But suppose they recognize us?" Mr. Catlett asked. "They warned that there wouldn't be a third chance."

"Then let me off somewhere close, and I'll go alone!" Josh cried impulsively. "We just can't leave Mom out there all by herself with those crooks!"

A brief silence followed as Mr. Catlett thought. He glanced at his wife. She shook her head.

"I'll go with you, Josh," Tank volunteered.

Roger added, "Me, too."

"Boys," Mr. Catlett said, holding up his hands, "that's very noble of you, but three kids would attract too much attention. That is, assuming I decided to risk following your plan."

Roger glanced nervously at Mrs. Catlett and the girls before speaking. "Excuse me, but a couple of haoles* might make those guys suspicious. But a local and a haole probably wouldn't."

"You'd go with me? Just the two of us?" Josh asked.

Roger nodded but didn't say anything.

Mr. Catlett frowned. "Josh, they might recognize you."

"The only one who's seen me is their helicopter pilot, and he probably wouldn't recognize me."

"We've got to do something to help Mary," Tank's father said as he sighed. "I'll risk it."

"I'll take care of the other kids and handle the senator," Mrs. Catlett offered.

Her husband nodded. "Josh, you'd better change, just in case the chopper pilot remembers the clothes you had on earlier. Then grab a couple of hats and let's go!"

A few minutes later Mr. Catlett's tires squealed as he spun out of the garage and onto the road. Josh's heart speeded up. What a trip this was going to be!

Chapter Seven

AN OLD FISHERMAN'S STORY

The rain had stopped and the skies were clearing, Josh noticed, as Mr. Catlett sped the car down the road. The boy also saw that the sun was rapidly sliding down the afternoon sky toward the vast Pacific Ocean.

"How far is this place?" Josh asked, leaning forward to look at Mr. Catlett in the front seat.

"I'm not sure. From the map, I'd say half an hour or so. You boys keep an eye out for somebody following us, or a helicopter. If you see something, sing out, and we'll turn back. No sense risking Mary's mission because we're spotted."

Roger took the right side windows and Josh took the left. Beautiful white cumulus* clouds were drifting along, left behind by the passing rain. In Hawaii, he had learned, it usually rained every day.

"Nobody behind and nobody overhead on my side," Josh announced after a minute's study.

"Same here," Roger sang out.

"Think we passed my mother somewhere, stopping for

70

gas?" Josh asked.

"I didn't see her. But since she has to stop sooner or later, we'll almost surely beat her." Mr. Catlett glanced in the rear view mirror. "I know her driving—slow and cautious; not like your father."

Josh grinned. His father was a careful driver, but he did push the speed limits. It was part of his nature, just as it was Josh's, to be in a hurry even if there was no reason.

Tank's father snapped on the radio. "Let's see what's happening with the eruption." He found an all-news station and turned up the volume.

". . .the evacuation of Pake is being carried out as a safety precaution, since the lava flow is moving straight for the village."

"That means it's getting worse!" Josh exclaimed.

Mr. Catlett turned down the radio. "The lava moves slowly enough so that everybody will get out safely."

"I'm having a little trouble understanding exactly where this eruption is," Josh admitted.

"Around on the other side of the island, closer to Hilo."

"Hilo? That's where Dad was going to take us later this week."

Tank's father reached for a map on the front seat. "Here's a map the car rental people gave me. It'll help you get oriented. First, find the Hawaii Volcanoes National Park."

Roger leaned over and pointed. "Right there. Below

and to the left of Hilo."

Josh studied the map, although reading while riding in a car sometimes made him slightly sick to his stomach. "Sure a lot of neat things marked here. Fern Jungle, Thurston Lava Tube, Chain of Craters Road. Boy! I'd like to see all those places, especially the volcano erupting!"

"You'll still get there, Josh. Just as soon as we get your father back, so don't lose faith."

"I won't."

"Good. Now you boys had better make another check of the sky. I can see nobody's behind us, so we're not being followed that way."

Both boys scooted down in their seats so they could see more of the sky and checked carefully. Both reported no aircraft in sight.

"Good!" Mr. Catlett said. He reached over to turn up the radio again. "Oops! What's that?"

"What?" Josh nervously demanded, leaning forward against his seat belt.

"Car's starting to steer funny. Look at the way the wheel's . . . oh, no!" He turned the wheel toward the side of the road and eased up on the gas.

"What? What?" Josh exclaimed, watching the car slowing in a wide, desolate area of countryside.

"I think we've got a flat tire!"

"You're kidding," Josh groaned.

"Know in a minute, boys." Mr. Catlett eased the car onto a small shoulder and set the hand brake.

Both boys were out their doors by the time the car came to a stop. Roger saw it first. The right rear was definitely flat.

Mr. Catlett ran his hands carefully along the rubber, then stopped. "I feel it. Nail, I think."

"We'll never beat Mom there!" Josh moaned.

"Can't help it," Mr. Catlett said, rising and brushing his hands together. "Let's get the trunk open and see what the spare's like."

The spare was not a real tire, but what Josh's father jokingly called a "kiddie car balloon." Mr. Catlett didn't have a much higher opinion of the spare. It was obviously made to get a stranded motorist to the nearest service station, but not much more.

"Well," Josh said, "I've helped my father change a couple of tires. Show me what I can do now, Mr. Catlett."

"Me, too," Roger said.

"You boys get the spare out, along with the jack. I'll take the wrench and get the lug nuts loosened on the flat. Shouldn't take more than about fifteen minutes."

He was wrong. The nuts had obviously been put on with an air-powered tool that was much stronger than Mr. Catlett. He strained and puffed but couldn't break the nuts loose. Josh and Roger tried while Mr. Catlett rested, but they couldn't do it, either.

Josh dropped the lug wrench and stood up, his hands sore from trying so hard to turn the tool. "Why'd this have to happen now?"

"Your mother will be all right," Tank's father said. "Here, let me try again."

Straining as hard as he could, Mr. Catlett's face turned red from the effort. Then a battered old Volkswagen approached from the opposite direction. Josh looked up while the tiny car slowed, stopped, and two huge Hawaiian men got out. Josh guessed each of them weighed at least three hundred pounds.

The young men grinned and walked across the quiet road. The first one said, "You malihinis* need da kine* kokua*?"

"I'm a kamaaina*," Roger said with pride.

"Us, too!" the first giant replied with a happy smile. He turned to Mr. Catlett. "Need kokua*?"

"Help? Sure do! We can't get the lug nuts loosened." He pointed to the wheel.

Josh followed the two giants around and peered between them. They grinned good-naturedly while the one who had spoken picked up the wrench. He settled it on the stubborn nut and gave a little tug.

"Hey!" Josh exclaimed. "You got it!"

The man quickly loosened all the nuts. Josh picked up the jack to slide it into place, but the second giant grunted and motioned the boy aside.

He gripped the car firmly and lifted it up. The other man removed the flat tire, slid the spare on and spun the nuts loosely into place. In a few quick movements, he had tightened the nuts. The other man lowered the car and brushed his hands.

Josh's mouth had dropped. The locals started back across the street.

Mr. Catlett, who already had his wallet out, extended a twenty-dollar bill. "Here, men! Mahalo*."

"Aloha," the first man said, waving goodbye.

"Wait a second!" Tank's father followed the men across the street, offering the bill to the first man, who pulled his hands back and shook his head. Mr. Catlett tried the second man. He also pulled his hands back.

The two Hawaiians squeezed their giant bulks into the tiny car, smiled, and drove off.

Mr. Catlett stared after them and said wistfully, "Now that's what I call the real aloha spirit."

Josh thought that was true, but the delay might have put his mother in terrible danger. He bent down and quickly grabbed the tools. "I'll get these things back in the trunk. Roger, can you lift that tire? Mr. Catlett, we'll be ready to go in a few seconds."

Slowly, the slender, wiry man turned and looked toward the sea. The sun was slipping rapidly off to their right, plunging toward the distant horizon. "It'll be too late by the time we get there, boys."

"What?" Josh dropped the jack into the trunk with a clang. "But we can't give up!"

"The idea was to get there ahead of your mother. If we come driving up now, we'll end up with the same problem we had earlier. You know what the caller warned would happen..."

Josh turned away in frustration, not hearing the rest. He knew it was true but didn't want to accept it. Yet he had no choice. He nodded in understanding.

Mr. Catlett drove more slowly back toward Kailua, not wanting to put any undue strain on the miserable excuse for a tire that rode on the right rear wheel. He flipped the radio on. The station was on a commercial break.

"Josh," he said, "you can't let this get you down. I'm sure everything will be all right with your mother."

The boy nodded, not at all confident that was true, but knowing he couldn't do anything to help her. He wondered what was happening to her right now.

He hoped she and his father were safely on their way back to the hotel. But it was possible that the captors had found out that the part of the video they wanted had been edited out and no longer existed. Would they believe that? Most of all, would they let Josh's father go free? If he could identify them—Josh shivered and tried to force his mind off the terrible thought.

Mr. Catlett seemed to sense Josh's fearful thoughts. He deliberately changed the subject. "Roger, what's this I've heard about your grandfather having an experience with the legendary fire goddess of these volcanoes?"

Roger was obviously uneasy, Josh saw. It was one thing to talk among boys his own age; it was quite another to say certain things to adults, especially newcomers to the islands.

"Go ahead, Roger," Josh urged. "Tell us about your grandfather."

Roger didn't say anything for a moment. He stared out the window. Slowly, he spoke. "He was a fisherman here on the Big Island."

He pointed to the map lying on the seat between the two boys. Josh followed Roger's brown finger as he found the spot near Hilo.

"I see it," Josh said. "But I thought your ancestors came from Japan to work on the cane* and pine* plantations."

"My great grandfather did that. I'm third generation born here. My grandfather didn't like the land, so he took to the sea. He was a good fisherman, my father tells me."

Josh's nature was high gear and fast moving, so Roger's careful explanation was too slow for him. "Yes, but what about this...this Pele?" Josh prompted.

"Grandfather had a big load of fish one day. He was unloading when an ugly old woman walked up. She had on a white holoku*.

"She said, 'Give me fish.'

"My grandfather answered, 'Go away, you ugly old woman! I don't have fish to give. I sell fish to the market.'"

Roger stopped and Josh urged, "Go on! Then what happened?"

Raising his eyebrows, Roger shrugged. "The old woman became very huhu*. She said, 'Come three days from now, Pele will destroy this village. Pele will destroy fishing grounds. No more fish to catch.'"

Josh was interested in spite of not believing in such legends. So was Mr. Catlett, for he urged: "Finish the story, Roger."

"Not much to tell."

"Well," Josh demanded, "was she supposed to be this fire goddess or not? Did her prophesy come true?"

Roger considered, frowning. "The old woman walked away from my grandfather and got in a Model T car. A Japanese man was at the wheel. He drove away while the old woman looked back and shook her fist at my grandfather. She repeated her warning, shouting so loudly he could hear her a block away."

Josh rolled his eyes impatiently. "Then what happened?"

"You Mainland haoles* are always in a hurry," Roger said, suppressing a grin. "Even to hear a story. But in Hawaii, no wikiwiki*."

"Roger!"

"Oh, all right, Josh! My grandfather said that after the old woman got in the car and the Japanese man drove away, he soon came back. Without her."

"Without the old woman?" Josh asked.

Roger nodded. "The man who had been driving the Model T told my grandfather that he didn't know the woman. She just got in his car, and he was so scared of her shouting that he drove off when she told him to. But he had driven only a little distance when he turned around to say something to her. Only—she was gone."

"Gone?" Josh echoed.

"Disappeared," Roger said.

Mr. Catlett asked, "What about the prediction the old woman made to your grandfather?"

"Volcano started to erupt. Within one day, the lava was so close to my grandfather's village that everybody started moving out."

"Evacuated the whole village?" Mr. Catlett asked.

"Took off the corrugated iron roofs, along with doors and windows and everything they could carry. Only the frames of the houses were left."

"What about the lava? Did it bury the town and the fishing grounds?" Josh asked.

"The Hawaiian people living in the village tried to make peace with Pele. They offered roast pigs. They offered awa roots*, raw fish and so forth."

"What happened?"

"The lava kept coming because Pele was so huhu*. Then a strange thing happened as the lava crept toward the village. My grandfather said that the lava began to make music."

"The lava made music?"

"Sounded like chimes," Roger said softly. "Or bells. Maybe both. A beautiful melody, my grandfather said."

Mr. Catlett asked, "Did the lava really cover the village?"

"Began burying houses the second day after the eruption. By the third day, the whole village was gone. Then the lava moved on and poured into the sea like a waterfall of fire. Lots of steam.

"My grandfather said that a photographer in Honolulu got pictures of that. They were printed in the paper. People said they could see Pele in one photograph. She was a young, pretty woman—a crown on her head—in the steam."

Josh wanted to laugh, but he knew better. From the look on Roger's face, it was obvious that he believed the story. Or at least part of it.

Mr. Catlett slowed the car and headed down into the hotel's underground garage. "Josh, isn't that your mother's car?" he asked, pointing.

Josh turned to look. "Sure is! But—how'd she get back ahead of us? And did she get my father?"

"No, she didn't! She's going toward the elevator—alone," Mr. Catlett said, pulling the car into a parking stall so hard the tires squealed.

Josh saw his mother turn at the sound. She started running awkwardly toward them across the concrete floor, her heels clicking. Josh leaped out of the car and ran toward her. "Mom! What happened?"

She opened her arms wide, threw them around Josh and collapsed in sobs against him.

Chapter Eight

A WILD IDEA

J osh's heart beat so fast he could barely breathe. "Mom, what happened?" he repeated. Then he asked the question whose answer he was afraid of: "Where's Dad?"

His mother pushed herself away from the boy to look into his face. "I don't know. His captors didn't show up."

"They didn't—" Josh began, but his mother interrupted.

"They sent another boy with a note." She released her son and fumbled in her purse. "Apparently they had someone watching our hotel room, because they knew the senator arrived."

"But he was coming to thank Dad for helping rescue his children!" Josh protested. "He came after you'd left, and he doesn't know anything about the tape or what's happened to Dad!"

"I know, but that doesn't make any difference to the kidnappers." His mother was gaining control. She handed Josh the note. "See?"

The boy glanced down at it, aware that Mr. Catlett had stepped close to read over Josh's shoulder. He read aloud: "What does the senator know? If you told him anything, you'll be sorry. Move to the Hilo hotel written on this card. Don't tell anyone where you're going. We'll contact you again. This is your last chance because our original twenty-four-hour deadline still stands."

It was printed in the same hand as the first note.

Josh gave a big sigh of relief. "Then Dad's still okay."

"I hope so!" Mrs. Ladd exclaimed. "But unless they call early, the time will be up!"

Mr. Catlett asked, "What hotel did he mean? Where's the card mentioned in the note?"

Mrs. Ladd plunged her hand into her purse and pulled out a business card. Josh glanced at it as Mr. Catlett took it.

"I know this place," he said. "Right on Hilo Bay. But it'll be almost impossible to get a reservation because all the tourists flocking to see the eruption will have booked everything in town."

Josh cried, "But if we don't do what the kidnappers said . . . !"

"Wait!" Sam Catlett held up his hand. "Maybe we'll be lucky and they'll have an opening." He turned to Josh's mother. "Come on, Mary, Josh. Let's get upstairs. I'll call the hotel while you two tell everybody what happened."

Nathan was waiting in the hallway when they got off

the elevator. The little brother whirled, opened the Ladds' hotel door and yelled, "They're back! But Dad's not with them!"

Everyone poured out the door: Tiffany, Barbara, Tank and Marsha. Then the whole group crowded around Mrs. Ladd, except Mr. Catlett, who went to the telephone.

It took Josh's mother several minutes to repeat her story. She showed the note and answered questions from Tiffany, Nathan, Tank and his mother. Roger stayed in the background, listening but not saying anything. When Mrs. Ladd had finished her story, Josh and Roger told what had happened to them and Mr. Catlett.

"The hotel's booked solid," Sam announced just as they were finishing their story. "But they already had reservations for the Ladd family. I also called some friends in Hilo. They invited our family and Roger to stay with them."

Barbara Catlett motioned for Mary Ladd to walk out on the lanai* overlooking the ocean. They closed the sliding glass door and put their heads together.

Josh noticed the sun, whose rays seemed to make a shimmering silver bridge across the water, was almost to the horizon.

"What's going on?" Josh asked Tank, jerking his head toward their mothers.

"My mom's telling your mother about the senator's visit," Tank began.

"The senator!" Josh exclaimed, "I forgot he came!

What happened?"

Josh sat down on one of the rattan chairs at a small table near the lanai. Tank took the opposite chair.

"Mom says he's a very sharp guy, and he got suspicious that something's going on."

Josh turned to look at his friend. "You mean because Dad wasn't here, or Mom, and nobody would tell him where they were?"

"My mom tried hard, but the senator asked some tough questions. When he saw Mom wasn't going to tell him much, he backed off. But Mom thinks he's going to do some investigating on his own."

"Oh, no!" Josh groaned. "That's all we need! You saw the note Mom brought back. Dad's kidnappers will know about it and think Mom broke her word. They seem to know everything."

"The senator won't be able to contact your mom again because we'll be at the other hotel, and the note said not to tell anyone."

"The kidnappers must want to make sure Mom's not working with the senator," Josh considered. "That's probably why they want us to move. Boy! I wish this was over and Dad was safely back with us!"

"Too bad we can't follow those guys the next time they set up a meeting place with your mother."

"You saw—they've got a helicopter and who knows what else. They'd spot us and then maybe wouldn't let Dad go."

"Yeah, I guess you're right. But I hate being so helpless!"

"So do I!" Josh thought how frustrating everything was. So far, every plan had not only failed but had also made things worse. Yet he didn't want to get discouraged. As long as there was a chance of getting his father back safely, Josh didn't want to give up hope.

"I wonder where they're keeping Dad?" Josh mused. "Maybe we could rescue him."

"Who knows? This is not only the biggest island in the chain, but it's also got all kinds of places to hide. There're mountains, jungles, desolated areas where old lava flows have destroyed everything, cattle ranches, caves, beaches, the ocean; you name it, the Big Island's got it."

"If we only had a clue!" Josh said with feeling. "Some idea of where they might be hiding Dad."

"Well, we don't, so you may as well forget that idea, Josh."

He sighed and nodded. "I guess so."

After dark, they checked out of their hotel at Kailua-Kona for the trip to Hilo. Mr. Catlett had made arrangements earlier in the day to get the flat fixed, so the silver sedan was ready to be driven again. The adults decided not to try caravaning because it was too difficult in the darkness.

Mrs. Ladd started off first in the black rental car with Josh, Tiffany and Nathan. The others followed some distance back in the silver rental sedan.

They crossed the Big Island to the northeast and came down the coast toward crescent-shaped Hilo Bay. Josh remembered his father telling the family about a tsunami* or tidal wave that had hit Hilo in 1960, killing more than sixty people.

As they neared the town of Hilo, the glow of the volcano erupting was visible inland to their right.

"When we get your father back," Josh's mother was saying, "we'll explore this area, especially the Hawaii Volcanoes National Park. It's not far from here."

Josh thought about a change he had noticed in his mother since this afternoon when she had collapsed in sobs. He didn't know what it was, but she seemed more calm, more confident.

His mother's attitude helped him get up the courage to ask the question that had been troubling him. "Mom, do you think they'll really let Dad go?"

"Of course!" She raised her eyes to the rear view mirror to see Josh. "Don't ever doubt."

In the soft darkness of the car, Josh didn't feel so sure. He didn't know how to express his fears.

"Is your brother asleep?" his mother asked.

"Yes. He must have been really tired."

"I'm glad he can sleep," Mrs. Ladd replied.

"I can't!" Tiffany volunteered. "I'm so tense inside I feel like I'll explode!"

Her mother reached over and placed her hand on the girl's shoulder. "We all have our moments, but I'm beginning to feel better. This afternoon, after Barbara told me about the senator's visit and his suspicions, I thought for a moment I couldn't stand anything more.

"I mean, the two meetings with the kidnappers went wrong, and their deadline was getting closer and closer. Then I thought of something God had promised, and I felt better."

"What's that, Mom?" Josh asked.

"There's a verse that says, 'Whatever you ask in prayer, believe that you have received it, and it will be yours.'* I've prayed many times since this whole terrible thing started, but this afternoon I really believed that promise. Of course, we also have to do what we can to make that happen and sometimes God has a greater good in mind than we can see. But I expect your father will be safely back with us very soon."

Josh wished he could feel so sure. He rolled the thought around in his mind as they approached Hilo. "Ask, believe, receive." It just seemed too simple.

Mr. Catlett had been right about the hotel; it hugged Hilo Bay. After the Ladd family checked in, Josh opened the draperies facing the water.

A spotlight shone on a glistening black lava tube*. He watched the water rise and fall in the tube. It was so peaceful and quiet, it didn't seem possible that not far away a volcano was erupting, and somewhere out in the darkness, his father was a prisoner.

Josh turned around and looked at the telephone. "You

think the kidnappers will call, Mom?"

"I'm sure of it. Please help me get your brother undressed while Tiffany hangs up our clothes."

Nathan was only partially awake and not helpful. He was like a half-empty sack and about as hard to handle. He was also grumpy and protested as they got him into bed.

Tiffany came through the door that connected the boys' bedroom with their mother's. "I wish they'd call! This waiting is driving me up the wall."

"I'd like them to call, too, dear. I'm sure they know we're here, but I suspect they're playing a psychological game of nerves."

"What do you mean?" Tiffany asked.

"The kidnappers make us scared by letting us guess whether they'll call or not; whether we'll be able to exchange the tape for your father before their deadline expires tomorrow morning."

"I won't be able to sleep until they call!" Tiffany exclaimed.

"Well, try," her mother said, pulling the covers over Nathan. "You, too, Josh." She kissed both boys on the cheek, reminded Josh to say his prayers, and left the room with Tiffany. The door closed behind them.

Josh looked around and saw a small television set on a swivel facing the bed. He snapped on the TV, turned the volume down low and began undressing.

A news story was on about how the volcanic eruption

had started. The woman newscaster was reading from her script. "Scientists at the Hawaii Volcanoes National Park were first alerted to the possibility of an eruption about 3:40 yesterday when an earthquake jolted the volcano area."

Josh moved closer to the TV, curious about how scientists knew when there was going to be an eruption.

The newscaster continued, "Scientists, checking seismograms* at Volcano Observatory after the heavy earthquake, found a harmonic tremor had been recorded for about two hours. A harmonic tremor indicates moving lava underground."

Josh guessed that meant the molten rock was moving up through cracks or fissures* in the earth. Eventually, the lava would escape by leaping high into the air as reddish fountains.

"The first eruptive activity," the announcer continued, "broke out about 5:20 a.m. in Napau Crater. This is some three miles into dense, junglelike terrain from the end of Chain of Craters Road."

Josh's head jerked up. "Chain of Craters? I saw that on the map. Dad was going to take us there."

The woman newscaster finished her background story and looked up, speaking without notes. "We're going to take you now by live camera to where our ground mobile unit has been set up for hours. They're following the threat of the lava moving toward the little abandoned village of Pake."

The scene shifted. A newscaster was standing in front of a small town. Josh turned the volume up higher to catch the man's words.

"Some of the lava is flowing into large crevices in this area, but volcanologists* tell us that unless something unexpected happens to divert the main flow, it will start engulfing this community sometime tomorrow morning.

"Of course, the lava will eventually pour into the sea and create more land. By then, this abandoned town is expected to be fifty feet under the flow. That will harden, and the town of Pake will forever be buried so deep nothing of it will ever again be seen."

"Wow!" Josh muttered. "Fifty feet!"

The camera tilted up slightly and began a slow pan of the background. Smoke, made visible by the distant fountains leaping into the air, swirled upward. On the ground, a river of lava crept down the mountainside. The melted rock was a slithering red-and-black mass that looked to Josh as though it were about a quarter-mile wide.

Suddenly, a terrible thought hit him. He snapped upright, staring at the screen.

"What was it the kidnapper said to Mom?" Josh tried to recall the exact words. "Something about, 'You follow orders, or we'll put your husband where he'll never be found.'"

Josh shivered, trying to shake the thought, but his eyes went back to the lava flowing toward the village. "What better place to hide somebody than in a town that's been abandoned because the lava's coming," Josh thought. "And if the kidnappers decide that they don't want any possible witness to ever identify them, all they'd have to do is leave their prisoner where..."

Josh shook his head hard to drive the thought from his mind. But it wouldn't go.

He went to the telephone and dialed the number where the Catletts and Roger were staying. He waited a moment after asking to speak to Tank.

"Tank? You know what you said about trying to follow those kidnappers?"

"Yes, why?"

"That may not be necessary. I've got an idea where they might be hiding Dad."

"You have?" Tank sounded excited. "Where?"

"The village that's going to be buried under lava. Tank, I'd like to get in that village and look around!"

"You're nuts! First of all, it's a wild idea. Second, I'm sure the police must have closed it so nobody can get in."

"Just the same, I'd like to take a look for myself. You want to come with me?"

"Me? I'm not crazy!"

"Listen, Tank, we could get in, look around and get out before anyone knows we were there."

"I can't believe you're saying this, Josh!"

"Then you won't go?"

Tank hesitated, finally saying with a sigh, "Well, I shouldn't, but if you go, count me in."

After Josh hung up, the feeling that he was right stayed with him. He undressed absently, his mind whirling.

Just before he turned off the television, he saw more pictures of Pake. The village was partially visible against the red glow of the advancing flow. The buildings looked totally empty and deserted.

"What if Dad's tied up inside one of those? Even if he could yell, nobody would hear him because everybody's left town. If the kidnappers don't free Dad tomorrow morning, that means they're not going to. And I'm so sure they've got him in that village that I've got to take a look! I just hope I can do it before the lava covers it."

He crawled into bed, but he couldn't sleep as he thought about what tomorrow would mean.

Chapter Nine

MYSTERIOUS FOOTSTEPS AT DAWN

The boy tossed restlessly in bed, trying to think about what to do. "Should I tell Mom that I think they're holding Dad in a village where lava's headed? No; that'd only scare her more, and I don't have any proof that's where Dad is.

"I'd like to check it out, but even if I could get into the town, where would I look? Dad could be hidden almost anywhere, and there wouldn't be time to search everyplace. The lava would get me if I stayed too long.

"Maybe I'm just scaring myself unnecessarily. Maybe the kidnappers will release Dad like they said they would when Mom gives them the tape. But if they don't, I'll have to risk looking in that village! Otherwise, if something happens to Dad, and I don't try everything I can think of. . ." The boy shivered, leaving the terrible thought unfinished in favor of another.

"I wish we had some help! Tank's father is willing, but he's not experienced in this kind of thing. And we don't dare bring in the police or anyone like that."

Josh wasn't aware of when the questions finally melted into nothingness and he fell asleep.

The phone's sharp ring in the darkness jerked Josh upright in bed. His heart beat wildly. For a moment, he stared into the blackness, trying to remember where he was. The answer didn't come quickly.

When Josh was awake, he liked to move fast, talk fast and think fast. But when he was asleep, he liked to stay that way. He usually slept late, woke up slowly and took his time getting out of bed. He especially didn't like being awakened by an alarm clock or a telephone.

The phone shrilled again. Nathan stirred beside him but didn't wake up. Josh muttered, "Who's calling at this time of night?" Instantly, he knew the answer: his father's kidnappers.

Josh heard his mother's feet hit the floor in the adjoining room. She apparently stumbled over something, for there was a muffled sound. Her footfalls stopped for a moment.

The phone jangled the third time. "Oh, no!" Josh moaned. He dragged himself out of bed and groped for the door that connected the two rooms. His mother had picked up the phone by the time he made it into her room.

"Hello?" she said, holding the phone far enough away from her ear for Josh to overhear the conversation. She didn't sound sleepy. Maybe she had been awake.

"Listen carefully, lady; this is positively the last time you'll hear from us."

Josh's mouth went dry, and he swallowed hard. He was waking up fast. He recognized the kidnapper's voice.

"I want my husband back!" Mary Ladd's voice was firm although Josh thought there was a little bit of a tremor in it.

"And we want that tape. But we're tired of messing around. Either we make the exchange this morning, or your husband will have a packing crate for a permanent home! You got that?"

"Yes, I understand."

"That's better. You still got the tape?"

"I have it."

"No copies been made?"

"No! Now, please tell me when and where to meet you—and my husband."

"I was coming to that, lady. Oh, by the way, you were a good girl to follow our instructions about changing hotels. See if you can do as well this morning. You ready for directions?"

"Go ahead. But unless I see my husband, alive and well, I won't turn over this video cassette. Is that understood?"

"That's what this meeting's all about, lady."

Josh didn't believe the man; didn't believe him at all. Something inside the boy warned him that the man at the other end of the line did not mean a thing he said—except that he wanted the tape.

"I'm listening," Mary Ladd said into the phone.

The man's voice seemed to have an echo, as though he were using a phone in a large, empty building. Josh listened silently until the man had completed his instructions and hung up.

After his mother replaced the phone, Josh asked, "Why'd he have to call in the middle of the night?"

"It's a trick to upset us. I told you these people are trying to make us nervous; keep us off balance so we can't think straight."

Josh saw his sister in a robe standing by her bed. She apparently had gotten up to listen when her mother talked to the man.

"I have the instructions on where to meet him," Mary Ladd said, pointing to a pad beside the phone. "If you're awake enough, I need to talk to you and Tiffany."

The mother and her two older children talked quietly while Nathan slept. Dawn crept up over the edge of the world before the three Ladds had talked through everything.

Josh stood by the picture window facing the bay and watched the light ease up over the distant horizon, followed by the sun. He watched the tide surge in and out of the lava tube* just outside the window. The strange sight began with a wave starting out in the bay. The curling blue-green water rushed toward the hotel, with most of the wave exploding into white foam against the rough shore where black lava had hardened centuries ago.

But some of the wave survived, rushed into the upright

lava tube* and shot out the top like soda water spewing out of the neck of a bottomless bottle. What sea water was left backed down into the tube.

"I can't get over it," Josh said, turning to look at his mother and sister. "Everything's so peaceful here—so beautiful —and yet this terrible thing with Dad's going on."

"It'll soon be over, Josh." His mother was already getting ready for the meeting, although the sun was barely up. "Your father will be safe in about three hours."

Josh nodded, but he didn't feel all that confident. He didn't trust the man, but Mrs. Ladd couldn't risk calling in the authorities until after the exchange. She'd assured Josh that she would contact the FBI the minute John Ladd was safe and they could reach a phone.

Sitting around waiting to meet the kidnapper made Josh restless. His natural high drive insisted he be doing something. But it was too early to call Tank and Roger.

"Mom, could I walk around the hotel grounds?"

"I'd rather you stayed here with me. I'll call room service and order breakfast."

"I'm not hungry."

"Me either," Tiffany added. She was already dressed but was still fussing absently with her hair in front of the mirror.

Mary Ladd looked at her son and understood. "Well, I suppose it's all right if you don't go far. Be back in half an hour, and don't wake your brother while you're getting dressed."

Josh was quiet. He pulled on casual clothes and tennis shoes. Stepping out of the room into a long, carpeted hallway, he noticed how quiet it was; nobody was awake yet.

Josh started toward the elevator, then stopped as he caught sight of some movement out of the corner of his eye. "Somebody's watching our room!" he thought.

That had happened before, because the kidnappers had known when the senator arrived. They were probably making sure Mrs. Ladd didn't contact the police. That also meant their phone was tapped and the kidnappers could listen to any call going in or out.

"Whoops! My call to Tank! If the phone is bugged, then they know where I think they've got Dad." Josh groaned inwardly.

He was tempted to turn and look to see who was watching the hotel room but decided against it. Instead, he tried to walk casually toward the elevator. Then he decided he didn't want to risk being alone with whoever was behind him. Josh noticed a nearby door marked "Stairs."

He didn't look around as he pulled the heavy door open and began walking down concrete steps that echoed loudly. Walking across a landing, he turned and started down the next level.

"Now!" he thought. "If somebody is really following me, he'll know I can't see him because I've passed the landing..."

The door above him opened quietly, but Josh heard it.

He kept going down, making sure his footsteps were loud. Maybe whoever was behind him wasn't really following him; maybe it was just an early-morning tourist getting a little exercise by taking the stairs down to breakfast. Maybe.

The boy was surprised how fast his heart was beating. He forced himself not to look back.

He wished Tank were with him. Or Roger. Or both. But they were probably still asleep. Josh kept going down four flights.

By the time he reached the lobby level, he had decided what he would do. Opening the door into the wide, spacious lobby, he glanced around for the nearest place to hide. A large potted palm tree stood twenty feet from the stairwell door.

Just beyond that was a television screen about four feet square. Josh caught a glimpse of the male newscaster, who was saying, "Scientists are puzzled over a second harmonic tremor detected early this morning near the abandoned village of Pake. This tremor indicates more moving lava underground, away from the present volcanic eruption."

Josh's quick glance showed no one was in sight except a uniformed hotel employee. He was walking away, carrying a tray of dishes. Josh darted toward the palm as the television newscaster continued in the background.

"Authorities were cautious in saying what this might mean, but did confirm that it is possible another eruption

is about to take place along some of the many fissures*
in the region of the present volcano."

In a few quick steps, Josh was behind the palm, holding
his breath, watching the stairwell door. The newscaster's
voice added, "If this theory is correct, a second eruption
close to the hamlet could bury it very quickly, before the
present stream of lava reaches Pake."

Josh grabbed the stickery palm fronds to keep them
from jiggling where he had brushed against them. As he
did so, the stairwell door opened. A man in a light tropical
suit paused, looking around.

Josh tried to still his speeding heart. He no longer heard
the newscaster's voice.

For about fifteen seconds, the man stood in front of
the door, glancing in every direction. He took a few steps
forward, looked again, then began hurrying down the
carpeted lobby after the hotel employee. "Hey, you! Wait
up!"

The employee apparently didn't understand he was
being addressed. He continued around the corner, the tray
held high. The man also disappeared around the corner.

Josh figured the man would ask the hotel employee if
he'd seen a boy. When the employee said no, the man
would rush back into the lobby to look some more. By
then, Josh would be gone. He had already spotted the
nearest exit. In seconds, he was through it and running
along a path of tropical plants in an inner courtyard.

"Now what?" he asked himself. "What'll I do?"

He thought of finding a phone and calling his mother, but she couldn't help him. "Think!" Josh told himself. "Think!"

He came to the end of the path and glanced around. This was obviously the back of the hotel, away from the bay. Well, that was better than being at the water's edge where there were fewer places to hide. But what lay beyond this end of the hotel? Should he hide or run? Run where? How could he get back in half an hour as his mother had told him?

Josh eased cautiously out of the beautiful garden of tall ferns, flowering plants and tropical shrubbery into an alley. The contrast was startling. It was like any alley in Los Angeles: narrow, smelly and scary.

"I wish Tank were here." Josh thought about calling but realized that wouldn't do any good. Besides, he didn't have any coins; he didn't even have the number where the Catletts were staying.

Josh tried not to be scared. But he was alone in a strange city, running from someone who might hurt him, and rushing to—where?

He stood uncertainly, glancing up and down the alley, his mind pinwheeling while he tried to think.

"Who is that guy? Why's he watching our hotel room? Hey! Maybe he was going to try to take the tape from Mom when she started out to meet the kidnapper!"

The thought scared Josh even more. "Yeah! He could grab it and run. Even if Mom struggled or yelled, he'd be too strong.

"Then they'd have the tape—but we wouldn't have Dad. We wouldn't know where he is. It's a trick! They never intended to let Dad go at all, probably because he could identify them."

Josh began hurrying down the alley, not knowing where he was going. He was just thinking furiously, and he didn't like the thoughts that came. But they were logical.

"The kidnappers had time to plan their escape. As soon as they had the video, they'd be on their way somewhere. Probably in the helicopter. Yeah! Even if they'd let Mom leave the hotel with the tape, I'll bet they'd have swooped down with that chopper, grabbed the tape and been gone before she knew what happened.

"Then they'd get to a commercial airport and take a big jetliner to some foreign country. Maybe to Tokyo; that's only about seven hours away. Or maybe to Mexico or Canada where American laws can't touch them.

"But no matter what, we wouldn't have Dad. What was it the guy said on the phone? 'Your husband will have a packing crate for a permanent home.' That was a strange thing to say. But there's no doubt what he meant!"

The boy's stomach seemed to twist and turn. The thought of anything so terrible happening to his father hit Josh so hard he wasn't careful coming out of the alley. He stepped onto the sidewalk without even thinking.

He heard somebody swear. Josh spun his head around and saw he had come out on another street that ran past one side of the hotel. He had also come right out in front of the man who had followed him!

Turning as casually as he could, Josh started walking rapidly away. He heard the man's quick steps behind him.

Josh tried to avoid running. After all, he was in a modern American city; a city where travelers were welcomed as visitors and never called tourists. Visitors were the lifeblood of the economy, so everybody protected them.

But nobody else was on the street, not even a passing car. There was just a boy being chased by someone who had kidnapped his father and obviously never intended to let him go.

Josh glanced back. The man was looking around quickly; probably making sure there were no witnesses. That was enough for Josh. He broke into a full run.

Instantly, he heard the man's footsteps as he also began running—hard!

"Hey, kid! Wait!"

Josh ignored the yell behind him. He raced down the deserted street, praying for a cop's car to come around the corner. But there was nothing except the sound of the man running behind him and closing in fast.

Josh sprinted with the speed of desperation, but the man was faster. His hands came down hard on the boy's right shoulder and spun him around. The man's arms clamped tightly around the boy.

"Gotcha!" the man cried.

Chapter Ten

HARD CHOICES

The man's arms were as strong as steel bands, holding down Josh so he couldn't move. But Josh's feet were free. He raised up the right one and brought it down hard on the man's toes.

"Ouch!" the man cried. "Kid, don't do that!"

"Let...me...go!" Josh managed to say as he struggled against the powerful arms.

"I'm on your side, kid!"

"Sure you are!" the boy exclaimed, trying to bring his foot down on the man's toes again. Josh's tennis shoes weren't as effective as leather soles, but he tried to make up for the difference by stamping fast and hard.

"I'm a cop!"

The words stopped Josh's movements at once. Cautiously, he raised his eyes to the man's face. "You are?"

"I sure am!"

Josh looked at the business suit and remembered something his parents had told him to do when in doubt.

"Show me some identification."

"I will if you won't kick me anymore."

"I won't if you're telling the truth." Josh figured that even if the man wasn't a plainclothes policeman, he would have to loosen his grip to reach for his wallet. That would give Josh a chance to twist free and run. This time, he would yell his head off. He'd wake up every malihini* and kamaaina* in Hilo.

The man held Josh's wrist with his left hand and reached inside his breast pocket with the right. He pulled out a small wallet-like holder and let it drop open. A silver badge glittered before the boy's eyes.

"It says 'Agent,'" he said uncertainly.

"An agent is a law-enforcement officer. It's like another name for cop, except I work undercover for a special federal investigative agency."

Josh relaxed. "I'm...I'm sorry, mister...officer, I mean, agent. I thought you were—"

"The kidnapper who's been watching your hotel room since they took your father hostage?"

Josh looked up and blinked. How did the undercover officer know about that?

The man replaced his badge holder and released the boy's wrist. "I'm Agent Fargo. I was assigned to guard your mother's hotel room last night. Our office took the man in for questioning who's been watching your room.

"Look, Josh—that's your name, isn't it?" The boy nodded and the agent continued, "Our department is cooperating with Senator DeMott, who is a very powerful man in Congress. We've been building our case against Lapser for months."

"Lapser?" Josh wondered just how much this man knew.

"We know Leopold Lapser is the man who snatched your father. We weren't quite ready to move against him; still gathering evidence. But he left us no choice when he took a hostage.

"The senator figured out that's what happened after he talked to your mother and then your family friend. Everyone was too evasive."

"But how could he have known that's what happened to my father just because he couldn't see him?" Josh wondered.

"Senator DeMott knew that Lapser had taken hostages before to exchange for what he wanted. He concluded that the same thing had happened to your family. Your mother was trying to keep the senator from knowing about your father's abduction. That meant she was trying to deal with his captors by herself, and so that's why my department was called in."

Josh bristled. "My mother's smart!"

"I'm sure she is, Josh, but she lacks the experience to deal with people like those she's up against. Now, if you'll cooperate, I can help your whole family get your father back safely."

Josh hesitated, studying the man's face. He was in his

middle thirties and starting to bald. His face seemed honest, and he sounded as if he were telling the truth. The boy said, "I want to talk to my mother."

"So do I. Come on! I didn't plan to leave her room unguarded, but your unexpected trip left me with a tough choice. I decided you were more likely to be in danger all by yourself than the rest of your family was in their room. But let's get back—fast!"

Mary Ladd opened the door when Josh knocked. Then she saw the man behind her son and gave a frightened gasp of surprise.

The agent had apparently expected that. He held the shield up instantly. "Let me in and I'll explain, Mrs. Ladd."

She hesitated, glancing at her son. "I think he's okay, Mom," Josh said. "He could have hurt me or taken me away if he wanted. And he knows about Dad."

Mrs. Ladd motioned the man and boy inside. The undercover officer glanced up and down the hallway before stepping into the room and closing the door behind him. He introduced himself and briefly repeated what he had told Josh.

Mary Ladd motioned the agent to a chair, but he shook his head. "Thanks, I'll stand. Mrs. Ladd, I've handled cases like this before. You're afraid that if you cooperate with the authorities, the kidnappers won't let your husband go."

He paused, studying her face before ending quietly,

"The truth is that they probably won't do that anyway, even if you give them what they want."

Josh's mother clamped her left hand over her mouth, and her eyes clouded with instant tears.

Josh swallowed hard, glancing at his sister. She was wide-eyed at the thought.

"I'm sorry," Agent Fargo added, "but that's the truth of it. Now, if you'll cooperate, there's a good chance we can get your husband back safely and catch his kidnappers."

Mrs. Ladd shook her head. "I don't dare help you."

"You don't dare not help!" the officer replied firmly. "Lapser is ruthless and will do anything—except keep his word. Believe me, the only chance your husband has is for you to cooperate with me."

Josh saw his mother's mouth working as she tried to frame the right words to say. Finally she said quietly, "Please give me a few minutes alone to talk this over with my children."

The agent nodded and went back into the hallway. Josh, his sister and his mother stood in a tight little circle before the window and talked rapidly. Their thoughts poured out as they expressed the various ideas that came to them.

Finally, Mrs. Ladd lowered her head and whispered, "Let's pray."

When she had finished, she motioned for Josh to open the door. Agent Fargo came back into the room.

"We've made a decision," Mrs. Ladd said quietly but

firmly. "God help us—we'll cooperate with you."

"Thank you, Mrs. Ladd. You made the right choice."

"I hope so! Now time is getting close for me to meet the kidnapper. He told me to come alone, so I've got to call some family friends—the Catletts—who'll stay with my children while I'm gone. Is all that okay with you?"

"Fine, Mrs. Ladd. Make your call. Then you'd better tell me everything, because we don't have much time. In turn, I'll tell you what our agency would like to do—with your cooperation."

Josh watched as his mother called the home where the Catletts and Roger were staying. "You're just leaving?" Mrs. Ladd said. "Oh, fine. We'll see you in a little while, then."

Josh studied his mother and the agent as they sat in chairs away from the window overlooking the bay. Fargo made notes on a small pad. When Mary Ladd had told him the whole story, he closed his notebook.

"Thanks. Now, Mrs. Ladd, it's time for you to get ready for the meeting with the kidnapper. I'll go downstairs and phone my office for some backup, then I'll tell you what I think you should do."

Tiffany said, "Use our phone."

"He can't do that!" Josh shook his head. "It might be bugged."

The agent smiled. "I won't be gone long."

As Fargo started out the door, Josh decided to tell him something that had been bothering him. He followed the agent into the hallway and closed the door behind them.

"It's probably just my imagination," the boy began, "but I've got to say it. I think they've got my father in the village that's right in the way of the lava flow."

The agent listened silently while Josh told him his reasons. "It's possible," Fargo said when the boy had finished. "I'll pass your ideas along to my superiors."

"Thanks, Mr. Fargo. Oh, there's one thing more. This kidnapper has a helicopter; a black one. Could they maybe fly down on my Mom when she's alone, grab the tape and take off? Maybe take her, too?"

"We're prepared for just such an eventuality, Josh. Don't worry."

"I didn't want to tell my mother because she might worry," Josh said.

"It'll work out just fine. Well, I've got to get downstairs and make my call."

Josh had only been back inside the hotel room about a minute when the Catletts arrived with Roger Okamoto.

"Boy, am I glad to see you guys!" Josh cried, grinning at his friends. "Wait'll you hear what's happened!"

While Mr. and Mrs. Catlett talked with Josh's mother, and Tiffany and Marsha discussed the latest news together, Josh brought his two friends up to date on events.

"Did you tell this agent about your idea that the kidnappers may be holding your father in that village?" Tank asked.

Josh nodded.

"You still want to go in there and look, don't you?"

"Let's wait and see what Mr. Fargo does," Josh suggested. "He just said he'd tell his boss."

"Dad had the car radio on while we were driving into town," Tank said, "and it sounds as if there might be another eruption about to start closer to that little town."

"I heard that, too," Josh said. "How close is the lava from the volcano that's been erupting?"

"Covered part of the village already. Just some warehouses and things nearer the ocean haven't been burned or buried."

Roger added, "The TV announcer said they'd start burning pretty quickly. By nightfall, the whole town'll be under lava; sooner than that if a second eruption starts."

Josh hoped his father wasn't being held in the abandoned village. "Right now," the boy said aloud, "Dad's probably with the kidnappers waiting to be freed when Mom shows up with the videotape."

"Let's hope so," Tank said softly.

When the undercover officer returned, Mrs. Ladd introduced him to the Catletts and Roger. Then the agent asked, "Mrs. Ladd, do you have the video cassette the kidnappers want?"

She nodded.

Josh thought of something. "Mom, is it okay if I take Dad's video camera when we go to get him? I can get pictures when he comes back with you."

"Well, I suppose it's all right, Josh."

Josh ran to get the camera from the closet.

The agent said, "All right, all of you walk out together. Mrs. Ladd, please follow the kidnapper's instructions exactly. Mr. Catlett, will you and your wife please keep a fair distance between your car and Mrs. Ladd's?"

"Anything you say, Mr. Fargo," Sam Catlett replied.

The agent continued, "Now, Josh, Tiffany and Nathan, you three ride with your mother for now. Then she'll let you out and go on alone, but don't worry. Either I or someone from our agency will be close by and have her under surveillance at all times.

"The Catletts and Roger will pick you up. Just wait together. When it's all over, we'll come back here and celebrate. Okay?"

There was a chorus of agreement. Josh was so excited his heart was pounding.

When they reached the lobby, the news was still being broadcast on the huge television screen. A fiery fountain of lava was spewing out of the volcano as high into the air as a six- or seven-story building.

Nathan stopped suddenly. "Hey, Mom! Look at that!" He pointed to the screen. "The lava's burning up that town!"

Josh saw that the camera angle had shifted from a moment ago. The telephoto lens now showed a bubbling black and red mass creeping across the abandoned village in a quarter-mile-wide river of molten stone about five feet deep. Buildings and trees nearest the volcano were already burning. Smoke boiled into the air, making a haze that drifted over the buildings in the foreground.

Wooden structures nearest the camera had apparently been part of the industrial area, Josh realized. Some of them had faded signs that could barely be read: Cannery. Fish Nets. Warehouse. Packing Crates.

"Come on, children!" Mrs. Ladd said firmly. "We don't have time to watch."

Josh gripped the video camera firmly as he followed his mother into the parking lot, but the scene on the television screen stayed in his mind.

At the parking lot, the agent turned and faced everyone. "Mrs. Ladd, you're going to be driving toward the volcanic eruption, but there's nothing to be alarmed about. Lots of people are out looking.

"Besides, my agency is pretty sure we know what the kidnappers have in mind, and neither the traffic nor the volcano will be a problem to them—or to us. Everything's going to turn out just fine."

Josh hoped that was true, but he was scared of what would happen to his father if anything went wrong. The kidnapper's time limit had about run out. And maybe his mother wasn't really going to be safe, either; not if the kidnapper was as ruthless as the agent said he was, and not if the kidnapper didn't plan to keep his word.

After some quick exchanges of encouragement, the Ladd family started out in the black car. The Catletts and Roger followed about three blocks behind. Josh didn't see what happened to Mr. Fargo because they were soon lost in traffic.

Josh thought everybody on the island was either flying overhead or driving along the road toward the volcano. The heavy sightseeing traffic slowed Mrs. Ladd down. After about an hour, Josh saw she was getting tense. She didn't say anything, but he knew she was thinking about the deadline. Would she get to the meeting place on time?

Josh was encouraged when he saw a sign for the Hawaii Volcanoes National Park. His mother slowed and turned off on a dirt side road.

"All right, children," she said as she stopped, "everyone out. Sam and Barbara are right behind us. They'll pick you up in a minute."

She got out as well and hugged and kissed each child. "I love you," she whispered.

Josh said softly, "Be careful, Mom."

"I will." She got back in the car and drove slowly down the dirt road into what appeared to be a fern forest.

Her three children stared after her.

Josh swallowed hard and thought, "I wonder if I'll ever see her—or Dad—again?"

Chapter Eleven

A LAST DESPERATE TRY

N ever to see his mother or father again? Josh shuddered and tried to drive the thought from his mind. He wasn't even aware that he still gripped his father's video camera.

Nathan made a little sniffling sound that drew Josh's attention. Reaching over, he patted his brother's shoulder. "It'll be okay. Mom'll be back in a few minutes with Dad; you'll see." Josh wished he believed that himself.

Tiffany turned around. "Here comes Marsha and her family."

Mr. and Mrs. Catlett drove up, got out of their car and spoke reassuringly to the Ladd children. As they talked, Sam put his hand on Nathan's shoulder while Barbara smoothed Nathan's hair. That seemed to comfort him.

Tiffany and Marsha walked a few steps away and stood talking softly. Josh, Tank and Roger moved a little way off in the other direction.

At first, none of the boys spoke. In the distance, Josh heard airplanes and helicopters flying visitors around the erupting volcano. Closer by, on the main road, Josh heard cars easing along. He knew they were filled with sightseers. Only these eight people waited anxiously for what the next few minutes would bring.

Josh glanced up at the sky. It was clouding up. That wasn't unusual, since nearby Hilo got around a hundred and forty inches of rain a year.

Tank broke the silence. "I guess waiting's about the hardest thing in the world to do, huh?"

Josh nodded but didn't answer.

"Your mother's going to beat the kidnapper's deadline okay, isn't she?" Roger worried.

Again, Josh nodded but didn't say anything. He didn't feel like talking. He ached inside with a terrible feeling he couldn't shake. Glancing in the direction his mother had gone, he saw no sign of her or anyone else.

Josh and Tank had been friends for so long that they sometimes didn't need to talk but could just be together. Roger was a new friend, usually shy and saying little. However, his nervousness seemed to make him talkative.

"You hear the radio driving down here, Josh?"

Josh shook his head.

"Pele really is huhu* this time!"

For a second, Josh was annoyed. He glanced at Roger, ready to say something about it being silly to believe in such legends. But Roger's face showed he was serious.

"How so?" Josh asked, trying to ease the annoyance he felt over Roger's remark.

"The scientists say that there's molten lava moving underground near the abandoned village of Pake. They're pretty sure that means the lava's following one of the faults, trying to find a weak spot to break out."

Josh didn't understand. He raised his eyebrows questioningly, still not wanting to talk.

"When it finds such a place," Roger explained, "there could be another eruption."

Josh frowned, suddenly interested. "You mean, near that village? If Mom doesn't bring Dad back, and he's really in that village somewhere, then if a new eruption starts—"

"Don't think about it!" Tank interrupted. "Get your mind on something else." He turned to Roger. "Tell us more about these legends."

"Well, the Hawaiians say Pele lives right up there on the edge of Halemaumau* Crater," Roger said, looking up toward the distant peaks. "It's half a mile wide. A big parking lot was built right there so people can look inside the crater.

"I've never been there, but once my parents and I walked in to another place near here. It was the strangest feeling! We walked across acres and acres of lava that had hardened. Everything was destroyed, except for a few small tree trunks sticking up out of the black lava fields. Yet my mother found some small plants growing in a little crevice."

Josh let his eyes drift to where his mother had vanished.

Still no sign of her. "How could that be? There'd be no dirt for roots," he asked absentmindedly.

"I don't know," Roger admitted. "But the plants were there."

Tank nodded. "I saw some little green stalks like that once when my family walked in to see an active crater. We walked for a long time over this rough lava. It tore up our shoes, and we thought we'd never get there. But we'd meet people coming back, and they'd say, 'It's worth it! Keep going.' And it was."

"Did you hear a terrible sound when you got close, Tank?" asked Roger.

"Sure did! At first, it sounded like a giant animal moaning in pain. Strangest thing I ever heard! When we finally got to the crater, it sounded as if the earth was alive and groaning."

Roger's dark eyes lit up with excitement. "And did the melted rock slosh back and forth?"

"Yeah! The pit was about the size of a football field. Looked a little like chocolate cake batter running from one end of a huge baking pan to the other."

"And when the melted rock got to the end of the crater, did it slosh up the sides and flare up in flames for a minute?"

"Yeah! Rocks so hot they had melted and were flaming! And when the wind changed, the sulfur fumes from the fire pit would make us all turn away, coughing and wiping our eyes."

"I'll have to go see that when my parents get back," Josh said, hoping such a day would come.

The silence started to settle again, and Josh didn't want that. It made the waiting too hard. So he said to Roger, "How fast does lava move?"

"Oh, different speeds. In 1950, I think it was, a flow was measured moving nearly six miles an hour. That one covered a village before it hit the ocean. I've seen pictures."

Even though talking helped pass the time, Josh's insides were twisting and turning. He was anxious to know that his parents were safe.

"Hey, look how low that helicopter is!" Nathan called.

Everyone looked up, but even as they did, Josh had a scary feeling. "It's the same one that we saw on the way to the City of Refuge! The kidnapper!" he cried.

Josh could see two men in the aircraft as it whirled overhead and started to ease slowly into what the boy guessed was a clearing in the fern forest. One would be the pilot. The other might be his father—or the kidnapper. Which one?

"If Dad's not with them..." Josh thought, his stomach seeming to tie itself up in knots.

Tiffany ran up, pointing and shouting. "It's landing right where Mom must be!"

The chopper sank out of sight, but the sound of the overhead rotary blades came clearly through the forest. Josh held his breath, wondering what was happening just a hundred yards or so away.

Suddenly, he heard a scream!

"Mom!" The cry exploded from the boy's throat. He started running along the dirt road, still gripping the video camera.

In the distance, Josh heard a faint cry. "No!" The word was repeated like echoes. "No! No!"

"Mom! Mom! I'm coming!"

Josh ran hard, unaware that the rain had suddenly started; unaware that others were running and shouting behind him. Josh's throat was so tight with fear he could hardly breathe.

He plunged into the fern forest, racing recklessly. He heard the helicopter's whine as the pilot revved up the overhead blades. A moment later, the chopper rose into the air, turned and flew rapidly away into the distance.

Josh dashed into the clearing that had been created by an old lava flow. The lava spread out before Josh in vast, black acres like melted black chocolate candy that had hardened into all kinds of lumps. It was rough, looking exactly like the molten rivers of stone he had been seeing on television. But the glowing hot redness was long gone, leaving only the blackness.

In the midst of it lay a crumpled form; one lone person.

"Mom!"

It seemed to take Josh forever to reach her side. He knelt, fearful of what he would see when he reached down and turned her face upward.

"Oh, Josh!" his mother cried, clutching his hands, "he knocked me down and took the tape! And he didn't bring your father!"

Josh had never heard such suffering in a person's voice. He tried to comfort his mother. Words poured out of him, soothing words, gentle words. He didn't know what they were; he didn't care. All he knew was that his mother hurt beyond any pain she had ever let him see before, and he wanted to ease that suffering for her. But only having her husband back would stop that for her and him.

Josh was only vaguely aware that the others were kneeling beside him. Mr. Catlett gently pulled Josh away. "Barbara will take care of her, Josh." The words seemed to come from a long way off.

Josh saw Mrs. Catlett kneel beside his mother. Tiffany and Marsha were there, too, reaching out, touching Mrs. Ladd. Tank and Roger were holding Nathan, who was screaming and flailing, trying to get to his mother.

Through eyes that were blurred with hot, angry tears, Josh looked up at the sky. The rain was coming down harder now, but Josh could still see the helicopter, which was carrying away the family's hope.

Then Josh spotted something else. He blinked, trying to clear his vision.

From high in the rainy sky, two military-type helicopters swooped toward the small black one. It tried to escape the larger aircraft coming in on both sides by dodging, diving and climbing rapidly. But the bigger choppers clung to the black one until it stopped swinging through the sky. Turning back toward Josh, it slowly eased earthward.

"Look!" Josh yelled, pointing. "They're forcing the black one down! It must be Mr. Fargo and his people."

The black helicopter landed. One of the military craft hovered just above the lava and off to one side. Josh saw armed men jump from the hovering craft and sprint toward the black chopper. The boy wanted to cheer as its overhead blades slowly stopped spinning. The other large helicopter rose again and zoomed straight toward Josh and the others.

It landed nearby. Mrs. Ladd was on her feet, trying to regain control of herself, when Josh saw Agent Fargo leap from the aircraft. He rushed toward the little group.

Josh ran to meet him, crying out the news of what had happened to his mother and the tape.

Mr. Fargo interrupted. "I know! We caught Lapser. Our men in the other chopper just radioed me that Lapser admits they have your father hidden in that village, but they won't say where!"

Josh blinked, sudden realization of what the agent meant hitting the boy like a slap. "We've got to find him, fast!"

Fargo shook his head. "There are a couple hundred homes in that village—or were! Part of them are already buried by the volcanic flow, and the others are catching fire from the intense heat. The whole thing's going to be gone in half an hour—maybe less."

"But my father's in there! We can't just leave him!"

The agent glanced at the boy's anguished face, then at the rest of the suffering Ladd family. "There's no time for a house-to-house search. But you're right—we've got to do what we can."

"Take me with you!" Josh cried.

"Sorry, Josh. It's too risky." Fargo turned toward the helicopter.

Josh ran alongside the man and grabbed his coat sleeve. "I've got an idea of where to look! Something the kidnapper said on the phone, and something I saw on television."

The agent looked down at the boy, then up at Mrs. Ladd. "Ordinarily, Josh, I'd turn you down flat. But we've only got a couple of men who can help. Mrs. Ladd, it's up to you."

She shook her head. "I can't risk it. If anything happened to Josh—"

"Mom, listen! We know Dad's in that town, and I think I know where to look for him. Please?"

"Mrs. Ladd," the agent said, "I understand how you feel. I don't want you to risk your son's life either. Excuse me; I've got to go."

"Wait!" The boy turned to his mother. "Mom, they've only got a few men to help look. They need me! Maybe just one extra pair of eyes and ears..."

His mother suddenly reached out her hand and grabbed

his. He saw tears in her eyes. Her lower lip quivered.

"Mom, please!" Josh cried. "I can help find Dad."

"Me, too!" Tiffany echoed.

Tank said, "I'll help."

"Same here." Roger nodded.

The agent shook his head. "Only room for two in the chopper. If we take anybody, it should be Mr. Ladd's son and daughter since he'd recognize their voices calling for him."

"Mom?" Josh cried in an agony of anxiety.

His mother gripped Josh and Tiffany in a quick embrace. She whispered, "God be with you!"

"Let's go!" Fargo cried, turning and crouching low, running toward the helicopter with its overhead blades still spinning.

"Coming!" Josh replied. He was so excited that he didn't remember grabbing the video camera. Tiffany raced beside him. They stumbled across the hardened black lava behind the federal agent.

In moments, Josh was buckled into a seat with his sister next to him. The helicopter lurched into the air so suddenly that his stomach seemed to fall while his body went up.

He had never been in a helicopter before, so he was surprised how fast it skimmed over the land. In minutes, it was passing over the end of the abandoned village nearest the volcano. Josh looked down over the river of melted rock slowly burying one edge of town.

Smoke and flames rose from the frame buildings that the lava had not yet reached. Only the large industrial buildings closer to the ocean still stood unharmed.

"Dad's down there!" Josh thought as the helicopter swung toward the part of town nearest the sea. "He's probably tied up so he can't get out. But we'll find him in time. We've got to!"

To ease his fears, Josh lifted the video camera, focused through the side window and began shooting.

The moment the chopper landed between the ocean and the edge of town, two uniformed men slid the side door open and leaped out. They ran toward the nearest building on the right side of the street. Josh heard them calling, "John Ladd! John Ladd!"

Agent Fargo jumped out next and turned to help Josh and his sister to the ground. Josh was surprised at the intense heat.

Whether from the lava or the burning buildings, or both, he didn't know, but the air was so hot he could barely breathe. His clothes felt hot enough to burst into flame.

The pilot stayed with the chopper, engine idling, ready to take off instantly.

Mr. Fargo yelled above the sound of burning buildings and the lava's movement. "Stay close to me! If I tell you to run back to the chopper, don't argue and don't delay. Understood?"

Josh nodded, gripped the video camera in his right hand

and began to run toward the nearest building on the left. Tiffany panted beside him, shouting, "Dad! Dad! Where are you?"

The kids ran past the agent who was looking in the first building. They raced on to the second building on the left, still calling their father's name.

Suddenly, Josh stopped so quickly Tiffany bumped into him. He pointed toward a weathered building halfway up the deserted street. A faded sign on the front read, "Crates."

"That's what I saw on television!" Josh yelled to Tiffany. It was a much larger building than he had imagined.

"Remember what the kidnapper said on the phone? Something about Dad having 'a packing crate for a permanent home'? I think that's where Dad is!"

"In there?" Tiffany exclaimed.

"Let's go see!" Josh answered. He broke into a run down the empty street.

He glanced upward at the volcano, still spewing out fiery fountains that slid down the mountain. The lava flow slithered like a black and red monster, destroying everything in its path.

Suddenly, Josh felt a sharp earthquake. He had only felt one once before, in Los Angeles a long time ago, but he knew instantly what it was.

He staggered, trying to keep his balance. He felt his sister's hands reach out to grab him.

"Tiffany, look!" he cried as he glanced up.

Some distance up the mountain, the earth burst open with a violent explosion that was instantly followed by a fountain of flame erupting from the earth. The lava slid down toward the Ladd kids.

"It's another volcano!" Tiffany yelled.

"You'd better get back to the helicopter! I've got to see if Dad's in there."

Josh turned and sprinted down the deserted street.

Chapter Twelve

WHEN ALL HOPE IS GONE

Josh ran to the warehouse, aware of the rusted corrugated roof above the sagging and weather-beaten sideboards. He tried to jerk the door open.

"Locked!" He shook it in frustration, then dashed to the side of the structure. "Got to find another door or window. There! A loose board!"

He kicked it off and squeezed through the hole, still clutching the video camera. The gloomy, semi-dark building was about a block long and was nearly empty except for some rusty pieces of machinery and hundreds of gray crates. They were stacked about fifteen feet high in long, silent rows running the length of the building. About three feet long and three feet wide, the crates had probably been used to pack fish a long time ago.

Everything smelled old, moist and smoky. Josh glanced up, thinking he could almost see the curling wisps seeping through the weathered cracks at the far end of the warehouse.

He jumped when a voice behind him said, "This place

128

gives me the creeps."

"Tiffany! You scared me to death! Why aren't you back in the helicopter?"

"I've got to know if Dad's in here." She cupped her hands to her mouth and yelled, "Dad! Dad!"

Both kids listened, straining to hear an answer. There was only the crackle of nearby burning buildings, the moaning of the new eruption in the distance and light rain falling on the high tin roof. The low throbbing of the helicopter's idling engines seemed more like a rumbling feeling than a sound.

"He's got to be in here!" Josh cried.

"But where? It'd take hours to search all those old crates and things!"

"Let's do what we can. You take the right side; I'll take the left. Hurry!"

Brother and sister split up and began running along the squeaking old wooden floor, calling out, looking behind the relics of boats, rusted machinery and anything they saw.

"Dad! Dad! Answer us!" Josh yelled, kicking down a stack of empty crates. They fell—slowly at first—into the vast, echoing space, landing with a noisy crash on the rough wooden floor. Tiffany did the same.

Josh looked behind the fallen crates. When the noise had died down, he strained to hear his father's answering hail, but there was none. Josh started running again, holding the video camera close and peering behind or into old barrels, pieces of rusted machinery and stacks of boards riddled with termites.

"Nothing!"

He glanced at his sister. She was nearing the far end of the warehouse. Behind her, hundreds of light wooden crates lay sprawled on the floor. Some still stood, towering toward the high tin roof, but there were too many to knock them all down in so little time.

Josh felt the earth quiver again. "Another earthquake!" He automatically reached out to the splintery walls to steady himself. Glancing up fearfully, he heard the ancient structure groan and creak. Pieces of wooden support beams fell, probably weakened by termites, which were everywhere in the islands.

"This whole thing's going to fall down on us," Tiffany warned.

"Dad's got to be in here somewhere," he called back, regaining his balance after the earth tremor. "Keep looking!"

"No!" Tiffany called, pointing. "The far end of the building's on fire! Let's get out of here!"

Josh was reluctant, but he nodded. The flames were already shooting up the tinder-dry walls and spreading toward them. It made Josh sick at heart to leave the building where he had been so sure his father was held captive. But the advancing flames and the swirling smoke left no choice. He followed his sister.

When he reached the board he had kicked off to gain

entry, he stopped and looked back one last time.

"Dad?" Josh called as he pushed the board aside so his sister could slide through. "Dad? It's Josh! And Tiffany! Can you hear us?"

Thump! A dull sound was faintly heard above the crackling of the burning building.

Tiffany stopped halfway through the board in the wall. "What was that?"

Josh spun around, trying to locate where the sound had come from. "Dad?"

Tiffany straightened up and pointed. "I think it came from over there. Look! A door!"

Brother and sister ran to the door and jerked it open. They stood in the entrance of what had once been a small office, their eyes adjusting to the darker gloom. Smoke was drifting in through a broken window.

The room was empty except for one large crate in the far corner. About five feet square, the box was made of light-colored boards. Josh thought it was probably much newer than the gray crates they'd been knocking down.

"Dad, are you in here?"

Thump!

Tiffany gasped and grabbed her brother's arms. "It came from that big box!"

"Dad?" Josh yelled, running to the box. "Dad?"

Thump!

Tiffany shrieked, "It's Dad! We've found him!" She ran toward the crate.

Josh bent over the crate. It had a lid. "Dad? Are you in there?"

Thump! Something hit solidly against the side of the crate.

"He *is* in there!" Josh cried. He whirled to face his sister. "He's probably gagged so he can't talk. Here! Hold this while I get the lid open."

He shoved the video camera into his sister's hands and spun around to grab at the lid. "Dad, we'll have you out in a minute!" Josh yanked hard, but the lid didn't give.

Then he saw the padlock. It was small but sturdy. Josh jerked on it, but it held fast.

"Dad, it's locked! I'll find something to break it. Tiffany, you go yell for Mr. Fargo and the others."

The smoke made her cough as she tried to answer. She staggered, coughing hard, out of the little office. She raised her voice and called, "Mr. Far—" but coughed so hard she couldn't finish the word.

Josh glanced around desperately for something to break the lock. There was nothing in sight. He ran out of the office into the warehouse and stopped in terror.

The whole building was on fire! Flames were racing along the walls toward him at amazing speed. The fire snapped and crackled as it consumed the old, bone-dry structure. Smoke made the boy start to cough just as he saw Mr. Fargo and his sister running toward him. The agent carried a length of pipe which Josh guessed had been a pump handle from some of the rusted machinery.

"Hurry!" Josh yelled, trying not to cough. "Hurry! Hurry!" He ran to the big crate and pointed at the lock.

"Stand back!" Fargo commanded, plunging through the office door toward the box. He swung the metal bar hard against the lock. It broke, sailing across the room. Josh helped Fargo raise the lid.

"Dad!"

The boy's glad cry was answered by his father's eyes lighting up, but he couldn't speak. His mouth was taped. His hands and feet were tied so that he sat in a partly-upright position inside the crate. His cramped quarters hadn't allowed him much room to move his legs, and his legs, crossed at the ankles, were bound with some kind of opaque plastic. Josh realized the thumping sounds he had heard had been his father kicking against a panel.

"Josh, grab his other arm!" Mr. Fargo ordered. "I'll take this one. Help me pull him out of this thing."

Josh was trying to obey when Tiffany cried, "Here come the other men! In here! In here! Hurry! Hurry!"

Two uniformed men dashed in and grabbed hold of the bound captive. The three men and the boy hoisted Mr. Ladd free of his prison. His hands were crossed at the wrists and bound behind him. One of the uniformed men produced a long knife and cut the bonds.

"He'll be too stiff to walk alone. We'll have to help him!" Mr. Fargo yelled. "You kids get out of here and wait for us at the helicopter."

Josh and Tiffany ran toward their makeshift entrance.

Behind him, Josh could feel the heat from the approaching flames. At the wall, he began to kick more boards loose so it would be easier for his father to squeeze through.

As several boards loosened, he grabbed them and started pulling them free. Tiffany put down the camera and helped tear the boards off.

"That's enough!" Josh exclaimed. "Get to the chopper!"

His sister obeyed. Josh slid through right behind her. They didn't stop until they were almost to the helicopter. Josh turned to see the three men right behind them, supporting Mr. Ladd, who was hobbling along as best he could.

Josh suddenly thought of something. He turned to Tiffany. "The camera! Where's Dad's camera?"

Her hand flew to her mouth. "I put it down and forgot!"

"I'll get it!" Josh exclaimed, sprinting toward the burning warehouse. He dashed past his father and the three other men, ignoring their startled exclamations.

The warehouse started to collapse at the far end. Josh saw it fall slowly, throwing up sparks. It was like dominoes falling, except the timbers groaned as they were wrenched loose, and the corrugated metal roof clattered down into the flames.

"Got to save Dad's camera," Josh panted.

He threw up his right arm to protect his face from the intense heat as he reached the warehouse. Bending down, he picked up the camera.

As he straightened up and turned around, he almost knocked Tiffany down.

"It's my fault!" she cried above the roaring of flames and crash of falling timbers. "Here! I'll carry it."

"No! I've got it. Get back to the chopper."

Both started running toward the helicopter. The overhead blade was spinning rapidly, although Josh couldn't hear the sound above the noise of the flames and the erupting fiery fountain. He saw his father in the aircraft. The three men were holding him back while he yelled, "Come on, kids! Come on!"

Suddenly, another earthquake under their feet made Josh and Tiffany stumble. A crack about five feet wide opened before them and spread out in both directions for about a hundred feet.

They slid to a stop, considering this new threat that had cut them off from the helicopter's safety.

"Can't jump it!" Josh yelled, looking around. "Got to go around. That way!"

Brother and sister turned and sprinted at right angles to the burning building. Out of the corner of his eye, Josh saw that the new eruption was still leaping high into the air. Two fingers of molten lava, divided by a slight hill, were pouring down from the fissure*.

"We're going away from the helicopter!" Tiffany panted. "We're going to get trapped between those two lava flows!"

"Got to get around the end of this crack!" Josh yelled back, clutching the camera to his chest. "Now! Jump the end!"

He saw Tiffany hesitate a second, then leap across. She staggered, caught her balance, and ran on. Josh was right behind her.

Suddenly, Tiffany stopped running and pointed. "The helicopter's taking off without us!"

For a second, Josh was also confused. Turning, he saw the twin fingers of lava begin to surround them. They were trapped on three sides, with only the open sea ahead of them!

"No!" Josh exclaimed, "They're coming to help us! Keep running! Run! Run!"

Tiffany did. And Josh ran behind her. The helicopter swung low, settled and almost landed. Strong hands reached out of the helicopter and dragged them in.

Seconds later, panting, scared but alive, sister and brother were helped to their seats and buckled in. Breathlessly, they told their father about the kidnapping details.

Josh stopped abruptly and turned to Mr. Fargo, "What time is it?"

The agent glanced at his watch. "Nine forty-five."

The boy smiled. "Made the twenty-four-hour deadline with a few minutes to spare."

"Too close to suit me," Mr. Fargo said with a grin. "Son, you risked your life for that camera. You just as well use it. Shoot!" John Ladd indicated the destruction taking place below.

Josh nodded and, with shaking hands, pointed the video camera at the scene below. He was still shooting when the chopper swung out to sea and the first lava poured over the cliffs. Great clouds of steam rose into the air when the extremely hot lava hit the cold water. Josh panned the camera slowly over the red and black mass still creeping toward the ocean; then back to the town.

But there was no longer a town. The warehouse and every building was gone. There was just a wide, black and red scar that had buried everything; a creeping mass that inched slowly toward the sea.

Even the small, fiery eruption that had broken through a fissure* near the town was gone except for some bubbling liquid that leaped into the air and fell back into the rest of the lava.

The whole scene faded into the distance before Josh pushed the Stop button. The red light winked off, and Josh saw that the helicopter was already starting its descent toward his mother, brother and friends below.

Josh looked up at his father and sister. "We made it!" he cried.

"Yes," his father said. "We all made it."

A few days later, the Ladd family was back in Honolulu with the Catletts and the Okamotos. The kidnappers were in jail. Agent Fargo insisted he had enough evidence to keep them there. The major national television and cable networks paid Josh enough for use of the video he had made of Pake's fiery burial that he bought his own camera.

The volcano legends were revived when some old Hawaiians insisted that in Josh's footage they had seen Pele in the rising steam as the lava poured into the ocean. One Honolulu television news director asked viewers to decide whether that was Pele or not. He made a freeze-frame to hold on the screen.

Roger then claimed he could see Pele. He tried to point her out. "See? She's an ugly old hag laughing over what the volcano's flow did to that village!"

Josh shook his head. "I don't see anything except steam." He still didn't believe in the legend. Neither did Tank.

Mr. Ladd was more interested in how he had survived his captivity. "I figured they wouldn't harm me as long as they didn't have that tape. But I had no idea they'd leave me in that place while the lava just ate me up!"

"See what I told you about believing and receiving?" Mrs. Ladd asked the children.

Josh pondered that, then said, "Maybe that's because when you believe, you take action on that belief, and God helps you to get it done."

To top off the family's celebration, Mr. Ladd's broker called with good news. He found a weekly tourist publication for sale at the same price as the community newspaper deal that had been lost. Mr. Ladd accepted the new offer.

Josh greeted this news with a big grin. "You mean we don't have to move back to the Mainland?" When his father nodded, Josh cried, "Great! It'll give us all the more time to tour the islands, and I can take pictures with my new camera."

"And your family can have more adventures," Tank added.

"I've got an idea—" the usually quiet Roger began with enthusiasm.

Josh reached out and smilingly stopped Roger. "Oh, no! After the trouble we had with your Pele legends, I don't want to hear another word from you!"

Everyone laughed so hard they could be heard half a block away. It was a nice feeling to laugh together, Josh thought. A very nice feeling.

More Trouble in Paradise!

Other Books in the Exciting Ladd Family Adventure Series

Secret of the Shark Pit

When Josh learns that his father has a secret assignment in Hawaii, his spirit of adventure is sparked. A cryptic map soon leads Josh and his friends on a race with a cruel stranger for priceless Hawaiian treasures. But the treasure hunt turns dangerous when the boys blunder into a shark-filled lagoon.

ISBN 0-8499-3899-6

Ghost of the Blue Lagoon

Josh and his friends don't believe the rumors of a ghost in the lagoon, but all the evidence seems to point to that conclusion. When they decide to investigate, they find that Hawaii holds dangers they never would have dreamed of. (Available June, 1989.)

ISBN 0-929608-19-4

PUBLISHING

Available at your local Christian bookstore, or write to Focus on the Family, Pomona, CA 91799.

GLOSSARY

Chapter One

Diamond Head: A prominent volcanic landmark.

Hawaii Volcanoes National Park: A park centered around the Kilauea Crater.

Kilauea: (*ki*-**lah**-*oo*-**ee**-*ah*) An active volcano located on the Big Island of Hawaii whose name means "spewing."

Menehunes: (*meh*-*nah*-**hoo**-*nays*) A race of tiny people in Hawaiian legends who are credited with building many temples, fishponds and roads. They worked only at night, and if the work was not completed in one night, it remained unfinished.

Pele: (**pay**-*lay*) A Hawaiian goddess of fire who supposedly caused volcanoes to erupt when she was angry.

Chapter Two

Anchorwoman: A woman radio or television announcer at a central station who coordinates broad cast coverage from various locations.

Broker: An agent who negotiates contracts of purchase and sale of real estate.

Dupe: (*doop*) to make a copy.

Guava: (**gwav**-*ah*) a sweet yellow fruit grown in tropical areas.

Papaya: (*pa*-**pie**-*ah*) a large, oblong, yellow fruit grown in tropical areas.

Roll: A term used by TV newspeople to indicate the playing of a tape—in this case, the transmission of the tape by way of satellite to the station, where it is recorded for later playback on the news.

Chapter Three

Bougainvillea: (*boge-in*-**vee**-*ah*) A tropical woody vine with brilliant purple or red clusters of flowers.

Da Kine: (*dah kine*) Pidgin for "the kind." This is more of an expression and is therefore not usually translated literally.

Oleanders: (**oh**-*lee-an-ders*) A poisonous evergreen shrub with white or red flowers.

Outtakes: (**aut**-*takes*) Part of a film or video that is not used in the edited version.

Plumeria: (*ploo*-**mar**-*y-ah*) A shrub or small tree that produces large, fragrant blossoms.

Shark Pit: This story is told in the first Ladd Family Adventure, *Secret of the Shark Pit*.

Chapter Four

Huhu: (**hoo**-*hoo*) Angry.

Kilauea: (*ki*-**lay**-*oo*-**ee**-*ah*) An active volcano on the Big Island.

Kilauea-Iki: (*ki*-**lay**-*oo*-**ee**-*ah*-**eek**-*ee*) Literally, "Little Kilauea." A small crater connected to the large one.

Pake: (*pah-kay*) A Hawaiian word originally meaning "uncle," but commonly used to mean a Chinese person. In this story, Pake is the name of a fictitious village.

Chapter Five

Buddhist: (**bood**-*uhst*) A person who follows the religion growing out of the teaching of Gautama Buddha.

Honaunau: (*hoe*-**nah**-*oo*-**nah**-*oo*) A former Hawaiian city of refuge where law breakers could flee for protection, which is now a national park.

Haoles: (**how**-*lees*) A Hawaiian word orginially meaning "stranger" but now used to mean Caucasians, or white people.

Monkey pod tree: An ornamental tropical tree that has clusters of flowers, sweet pods eaten by cattle, and wood used in carving.

Ohana: (*oh*-**haw**-*nah*) A Hawaiian term for evening devotions. The term literally means "a family."

Pandanus: (*pan*-**dah**-*noos*) A fiber made from the

leaf of the pandanus plant and used for woven products such as mats and hats.

Pupule: (*poo*-**poo**-*lay*) Crazy.

Chapter Six

Haoles: (**how**-*lees*) Caucasians; whites.

Chapter Seven

Awa roots: (**ah**-*vah* roots) Roots of a shrub of the pepper family.

Cane: Sugarcane.

Cumulus clouds: (**kue**-*ma*-*lus* clouds) A cloud form with a flat base and rounded outlines piled up like a mountain.

Da kine: (*dah kine*) Pidgin for "the kind," not usually translated literally.

Haoles: (**how**-*lees*) Caucasians; whites.

Holoku: (**hoe**-*low*-**coo**) A dress or gown with a train.

Huhu: (**hoo**-*hoo*) Angry.

Kamaaina: (*kham*-*ah*-**eye**-*nah*) A Hawaiian word meaning "child of the land," or native.

Kokua: (*koe*-**coo**-*ah*) Help.

Mahalo: (*maw*-**hah**-*low*) Thanks.

Malihinis: (*mahl*-*ee*-**hee**-*nees*) Newcomers.

Pine: Pineapple.

Wikiwiki: (**wee**-*kee*-**wee**-*kee*) Hurry.

Chapter Eight

Fissures: (**fish**-*urz*) Narrow openings or cracks of considerable length and depth.

Lanai: (*lay*-**nay**-*ee*) A patio, porch, or balcony. Also, when capitalized, a smaller Hawaiian island.

Lava tube: A tube of lava that is formed when the outside lava hardens into a crust through which the hot, interior lava flows. Eventually, most of the lava drains out of the inside, leaving a tunnel or tube. These may be up to fifty feet in diameter.

Mark 11:24, RSV: The verse Josh's mother quotes.

Seismograms: (**size**-*ma-grams*) The record of an earth tremor by a seismograph, an apparatus that measures vibrations in the earth.

Tsunami: (*soo*-**nam**-*ee*) A tidal wave produced by a volcanic eruption.

Volcanologists: (**vol**-*kan-all-a-justs*) scientists who study volcanoes.

Chapter Nine

Fissures: (**fish**-*urz*) Narrow openings or cracks of considerable length and depth.

Lava tube: A tube of lava that is formed when the outside lava hardens into a crust through which the hot, interior lava flows. Eventually, most of the lava drains out of the inside, leaving a tunnel or tube. These may be up to fifty feet in diameter.

Chapter Ten

Kamaaina: (*kham-ah-**eye**-nah*) Native-born.
Malihini: (*mah-lee-**hee**-nee*) Newcomer.

Chapter Eleven

Halemaumau Crater: (*hahl-**lay**-mau-mau*) A volcano of Kilauea. The term literally means "fire pit."
Huhu: (**hoo**-*hoo*) Angry.

Chapter Twelve

Fissure: (**fish**-*ur*) A narrow opening or crack of considerable length and depth.